Sands of the Prophet

THE DARK FILAMENT EPHEMERIS
EPHEMERIS
VOLUME III

RUSSELL C. CONNOR

DARKFILAMENT.COM

Contact the author at
facebook.com/russellcconnor
Or follow on Twitter @russellcconnor

Cover Art by SaberCore23 Artwork Studio
For commissions, visit sabercore23art.com

ISBN:
978-1-7331133-9-7

First Edition: 2020

Praise for Russell C. Connor's Work:

Good Neighbors

"Connor's ability to richly develop each character and plot thread is fascinating even when the horror is reserved... the constricting pressure as the dread piles on makes this book hard to put down and even harder to go to sleep after reading. This is a great novel..."
-David J. Sharp, *Horror Underground*

Second Unit

"Intricately plotted and vividly layered with suspense, emotional intensity and strategic violence."
-Michael Price, *Fort Worth Business Press*

"Drips with eeriness...an enjoyable book by a promising author."
-Kyle White, *The Harrow Fantasy and Horror Journal*

Finding Misery

"Major-league action, car chases, subterfuge, plot twists, with a smear of rough sex on top. Sublime."
-Arianne "Tex" Thompson, author of *Medicine for the Dead* and *One Night in Sixes*

The Jackal Man

"Connor delivers a brisk, action-packed tale that explores the dark forests of the human--and inhuman--heart. Sure to thrill creature fans everywhere."
-Scott Nicholson, author of *They Hunger* and *The Red Church*

Also by Russell C. Connor

For Taylor and the rest of the Esco Clan
For their friendship and
unwavering support.

And special thanks to Christina Pike, for helping
out a stranger.

TABLE OF CONTENTS

Laerz twisted the wooden club in his sweating hands as he crouched next to the shattered front window of the building. He believed the place had once been a roadside eatery of some sort, one with polymer booths and tables affixed to the walls, a kitchen full of bewildering chromium appliances, and a long merchant counter above which were mounted pictures of the establishment's strange offerings, the most prevalent seeming to be crusted tubes called 'French fries.' Now it was just another crumbling, old-world structure, full of dust and rust and the stagnant promises of a better age. He wished he could secure the place, if only to board up the gaping windows, but there had barely been time to grab a weapon from the rubble.

Behind him, deeper in the cobwebbed shadows, his wife Carmeel huddled with their seven-year-old son and four-year-old daughter in her arms. Both children shivered with fear against her shoulders as she clutched them. Her eyes found his in the darkness; Laerz could see the glaze of terror in them. He gave her the most reassuring nod he could muster before raising up to peek through the glass-sharded casement and assess their situation.

A crete lot surrounded the building, marked with a faded grid to show where autos had once parked while their owners came inside. On the far side of the gray expanse, beneath the giant yellow arches that lorded over the eatery, twelve Incarnates on horseback congregated.

Far too many for him to even consider fighting. His heart sank.

The demons had picked up their scent three days ago, outside a town called Saint Samsung, where Laerz and his family were granted permission to spend a single night. It was a common boon offered to families on a Rearing, at least in the smaller settlements, and the couple relied heavily upon these brief sanctuaries so they could catch a decent night's sleep. This migrational life wasn't easy, but with help from those brave enough to defy the Filament, survival was possible. Laerz and Carmeel had been running seven years now, since the night their son was born, and never regretted the decision. They'd experienced several close brushes with Incarnates, but Laerz had developed some reliable methods for confusing their keen tracking abilities.

Not this time, however. He'd spotted the first pair following them from a distance over the grassy hills, nothing more than a couple of sunrotted roamers. After a few evasive maneuvers, it seemed that Laerz was putting distance between them and his family. Then several more joined the hunt the next morning, sweeping in from the north to cut them off, followed by another two that came riding out of the east. Soon an entire pack of the red-eyed demons were hot on their heels, and he just couldn't shake them. From the way they anticipated his every tactic, it was as if these Incarnates were reading his mind rather than merely sensing the children. Laerz and his family were forced to outright flee as the posse closed in, staying on the move day and night. When the exhaustion grew too severe, they took refuge in the first shelter they could find beside an empty stretch of ancient road.

The Incarnates milled outside the eatery, speaking amongst themselves. One of them—the leader, judging by the others' deference to him—had two leashes tied to the pommel of his saddle. At the opposite end of these ropes were two grotesque, knee-high creatures that looked like squishy black wads with a thousand purple tentacles beneath. Both strained at the limit of their restraints in the direction of the building, as still and unflinching as statues. Laerz wondered if these bizarre hunting dogs were the reason he hadn't been able to lose their pursuers.

As he watched, the demons shared a laugh about something, their voices as harsh and raspy as a wire brush dragged across wood, then the leader dismounted and strutted a few paces closer to the building.

"We know you're in there," he called. He was a lanky specimen, eyes covered by smoke-tinted shards of glass jammed into spectacle frames, dressed in denim dungarees and a plaid jerkin. He wore rudimentary armor also, peeling leather pauldrons and bracers studded with rusted nails. Sunrot had taken root at the base of his throat, spreading up his neck in black tendrils of putrid flesh. "And you know what we want."

"*Leave us alone!*" Laerz shouted, dismayed to hear shrill panic in his voice.

The Incarnate threw back his head and barked cruel laughter. "It's far too late for that, mortal! If you wanted us to leave you in peace, you never should've created those two vile Lightbringers in the first place!" The demons behind him joined in the jeering. He waited for their amusement to taper before continuing. "But there is no need for you all to die today. I will make you a deal. Send your children out to me, and, if you agree to watch what we do to them, you and your sin cow woman may go free."

Behind Laerz, Carmeel let out an anguished sob. This was what they'd feared since their desperate Rearing began, the nightmare that had plagued them for seven years, the unspeakable possibility they'd only dared discuss late at night, after the children were asleep. And yet, even with all that dreadful forethought, the end had still come upon them far more suddenly than he ever could've imagined. Laerz crawled closer to his family, gathered them into his arms, and kissed the tops of each of their heads.

As he pulled away, Carmeel arched her eyebrows with an unspoken question. Laerz nodded.

"What say you to my generous offer?" the Incarnate prompted.

"*Go to hells!*" he howled over his shoulder. "*You touch my children, and I'll kill you all!*"

"Oh, we'll see about that, mortal."

With difficulty, Laerz released his loved ones and scrambled back to the window to crouch with the club. Tears blurred his vision, but he would do his best to take one or two of these bastards out of the world if they stormed the eatery. Carmeel wept loudly at his back. He knew she would be removing the pouch of powered drawken vine she kept in her blouse, preparing to give each of the children a spoonful.

Better that their darlings fade painlessly into eternal slumber than face the atrocities the Incarnates would subject them to.

From outside, he could hear movement. The whinny of horses. Muffled voices that sounded increasingly angry. Laerz waited, the wooden club cocked back to swing, muscles aching with tension, but none of the demons came. Finally, he heard the hollow clatter of departing hoofbeats on the hard crete. He held out a hand to stay Carmeel—she paused with a measure of greenish-brown powder cupits away from their son's lips—and looked through the window.

Ten of the Incarnates were riding away at full gallop. The leader appeared to be arguing with the last one, who gestured after the others. Then this one turned and urged his horse away as well, while the leader bared his teeth, clenched a fist, and climbed back onto his own mount.

"Today is your lucky day, mortal!" the Incarnate snarled. "We have been summoned, along with every other *Exatraedes* across this misbegotten land! There are bigger fish than you that must be gutted!" He leaned off the horse, and his glass-covered eyes stared right at Laerz. "Rest assured though…we will find you again. And we will not be so merciful next time."

With this threat delivered, he rode hard after his brethren, the tentacled creatures half-scurrying, half-dragged behind him.

Relief threatened to melt Laerz into a puddle. He let the club fall from his fingers and went back to his family. They sat on the floor of the eatery for a long time, holding hands. Carmeel and the children eventually dropped into weary sleep, but Laerz stayed awake for a while longer. He couldn't stop wondering about this person that had saved his children, and what they'd done to deserve such urgent pursuit by so many Incarnates.

Whoever they were, Laerz wished them a speedy flight and a painless escape.

The Valley of Bones

THE WORLD ANEW

1

Korden's artcraft shield had protected Gwenita from most of the shots fired by the Incarnates that ambushed them outside Ida. But an errant projectile had slipped past him to pierce the bonnet, leaving behind a round, thumb-sized hole in the polymer and tearing through the meat of Lillam's left arm, just below the shoulder. Korden remembered hearing her scream during the chase but didn't realize the extent of her injuries until after their frantic escape. She lay on the vehicle's floor, moaning in pain, as Rand tried to staunch the bleeding. Korden knelt beside him and reached for her.

"*Don't touch me!*" she shrieked, shrinking away from his hands. Sweat coursed down her pain-scrunched face as she glared at him.

"But I might be able to help the—"

"I don't want *your* help. Your filthy magic might get in the blood and infect my baby."

He stared at her in blank shock, unable to respond. Rand gave him an uneasy look and said, "It's all right. I'll see what

I can do. Just...give us some space." After Korden moved away, the man grabbed the room divider he'd created by hanging a sheet from the ribs of the bonnet and pulled it around him and his woman, sealing them out of sight.

Meech put a hand on Korden's shoulder and turned him around. "Don't fret on, li'l drude. It's *her* problem, not yours."

Korden nodded numbly. He'd faced plenty of prejudice as both a Crafter *and* a pre-ager since leaving the village, but Lillam's outburst had been the worst vitriol aimed directly at him since his encounter with Merise. However, as much as the words stung, he couldn't find the energy to dwell on them.

Because so much of his attention was occupied with another matter.

Heater Kay was *alive*.

This fact burned inside Korden's brain, impossible to ignore. The man responsible for Winstid's death—along with a good chunk of the other elderly residents of Hidden Glen—had survived a high-speed crash and swallowing a fireball shoved down his throat by Korden. Worse than that, the Triker had freed the multi-conscioused entity known as Loathe from its stone arch prison deep within the redwood forest. Two of Korden's worst enemies had joined together, not just philosophically but in a very literal, *physical* sense, giving each other access to untold levels of power. He could close his eyes and see the way the man's fingers grew like fleshy vines, the swarm of horrible insects that bore his bearded likeness, the energy projectiler that appeared in his hand. Upper only knew what else they could conjure.

And, as if all that weren't terrible enough, it appeared that Heater had somehow enlisted the Incarnates to help hunt Korden down. The implications terrified even Stone.

His weariness must've shown, judging by Meech's next words. "Why don't you get some sleep? You've hardly even sat down since yesterday morning."

"I have to keep an eye on Doaks," he argued, flapping a hand toward the control deck at the front of the wagon, where the squat little trickster sat hunched over the various levers and dials that controlled Gwenita. "We have to be careful around him. He could have a button that'll toss us all out the back of this thing."

"Naw, he'd've used it by now if he did. It's kye though, I'll stand guard over Doc Framface."

Korden hesitated. "Are you sure?" he asked, then rushed to clarify, "I mean, you're probably tired, too..."

Meech gave his lopsided, sheepish grin, but his aura flushed with a deep shame. The man still hadn't gotten over his resentment at being left behind when Korden went to retrieve the batteries for the wagon. "I slept all day, remember? I can do this, I swear. All I gotta do is keep 'im pointed east, right?"

"For now, I guess. We can figure out where we're going in the morning, after we put some distance between us and the Incarnates." He was reluctant to hand the job over to anyone, let alone Meech, but he couldn't very well watch Doaks by himself the whole journey. Besides, if the man truly wanted to be his 'bodyguard,' then he had to be shown trust at some point. And, after all, it'd been him who liberated Doaks from Ida's detention cells in the first place. "But you might want to tie his hands to the console or something. Just in case."

"Can do, drude." Meech's smile became devilish. "I'll even make sure to leave the ropes loose enough so he can use a couple of his fingers."

With that taken care of, Korden grabbed his bedroll from the carry pouch and headed onto the rear deck of the wagon. Doaks had slowed their pace considerably now that the chase was over, reducing the wild rocking and screeching wind around the hovering vehicle. Slender-trunked aspens pressed in on both sides, their leaves tinged a pale silver by the moon. The wooded trail was dark and empty as it unspooled behind them, but Korden watched it for a long time anyway, expecting to see the flicker of lights or hear the baritone rumble of a hovertrike. That they never appeared did little to soothe his nerves.

Heater Kay—and the malevolent, reality-defying entity inside him—would not give up. They would be keep coming, one way or another.

Korden instructed Stone to engage his alarm setting and spread his bedroll on the deck, but it wasn't until he climbed inside that he remembered Zeega. He couldn't recall seeing the small riftling since she'd leapt aboard the wagon into his arms after killing the last of their Incarnate pursuers and disabling Heater's ride. He started to get back up to look for her, then caught sight of one purple tentacle draped over the the edge of the bonnet above his head.

She was perched on the arched roof, staring upward at the stars visible through the tree canopy. Something about her tense posture made him decide against disturbing her.

But he was surprised to find her presence oddly comforting as he laid his head down and dropped immediately into slumber.

2

Over the past few weeks, Korden had experienced a series of strange dreams in which people from his past encouraged him—by way of very infuriating rhyming couplet—to keep moving east as fast as possible, sometimes at the expense of all else. They claimed he would be safe only after he'd crossed the Valley of Bones and arrived at the long mountain range known as 'the Skyreach' that bisected this land. He'd argued with Stone often about whether these might be messages sewn into his subconscious from the Upper, but, in any case, Korden woke from these sleeping delusions utterly refreshed and overwhelmed with artcraft, so he certainly hadn't dreaded them.

When the familiar dream started this time, he found himself in Winstid's cozy log cabin back in Hidden Glen. The Peacekeep himself sat in front of the fireplace where he and Korden shared a drink an eternity ago. Usually, a deep sense of euphoric calm pervaded all other emotion during these visions. Now, however, a wrenching spike of grief hammered through Korden's chest at the sight of the man, who had died saving him from Heater in the real world. Winstid turned in the seat to study him, his dark face set in a scowl, then brusquely waved at the rocking chair beside him. Korden crossed the room and eased into it, every part of him filled with a twitching tension.

"Back to causin trouble for decent folk, I see," Winstid groused. Firelight caused the skin growths spread across his dark face to stand out in detail far too intricate for a dream. "Guess it wasn't enough that you took everything from me."

"That's not fair!" Korden argued. "I never meant to hurt anyone! *You're* the one who dragged me back to your town!"

"*Fair? Meant to?* Well, that makes it all hunky-dory!" The sarcasm was so biting, it made Windstid's upper lip curl like the rind of a panka fruit left too long in the sun. "Why don't you ask the people of Ida what they think of your sob story?"

Korden's vision wavered with tears as he thought about Mayor Hildan and the rest of the townsfolk in the settlement they'd just left. These poor people would be punished by the Filament for harboring him, even though the truth was far more complicated than that. "I left as fast as possible, so I could lead the Incarnates away. I don't want anyone getting hurt because of me, but I can't just entirely avoid—"

Winstid cut him off with a grunt before delivering his next accusation. "And yet, if you'd listened to what you were tol', there'd be no need for this rigamarole!"

"W-what? What do you mean?"

"Don't act innocent, or play me for dim!" He jabbed a finger at Korden's nose. "You should've kept movin…but you waited for *them*!"

There was no need to ask who he meant. "They're my… my friends," Korden said, trying to convince even himself that such a label applied to the ragtag, disparate group travelling with him. "They needed help. All of them. I couldn't turn my back on them."

The Peacekeep blew air through his lips and flapped a dismissive hand. His next words held a venomous loathing that the real man had never been surly enough to affect. "They're dead weight; just holdin you back. Leave them behind...and get along on the path."

Korden saw it then. A picture mounted above the fireplace, the same one that had been on the wall of Bibb's *hucté*, in the dream Korden had outside Tay-Ho. The two shadowy figures in the foreground appeared to be a little more in focus this time. He stood up from his chair and moved toward the painting, keeping his eyes on the image as he asked, "You're not the Upper...are you?"

"Never said I was, boy. Never claimed to be." Winstid's tone softened considerably behind him, becoming almost reverent. "But *those* are two people who can do far more for you than He."

Korden reached the hearth and stared up at that picture, the majestic mountains in the background—surely somewhere in the Skyreach, with one slanting peak in particular standing out among the others—and those two shapely figures with their hands around each other's waists standing in the long umbra cast by the peaks. Not only were their silhouettes more defined, as if accenting the voluptuous bodies, but they shone brighter as well, enough for a hint of smiling faces to show through. Their skin hues were so dark that he suspected they might be blackenfolk, like the man behind him. His stomach fluttered with a breathless, yearning excitement as he beheld them, causing the crotch of his dungarees to tighten.

"Who are they?" he asked dreamily. The cabin suddenly seemed fake and hollow around him. He felt like he could knock the walls down merely by touching them.

"Ones who've been waiting a long time for you," Winstid answered gravely. "Ones who will help you remake this world anew."

ASKING QUESTIONS

1

When sunrise came, it found them cupiting their way down off the far eastern slopes of the Sierras into a hilly low country overrun with dangerously high thickets of skilne that grabbed at the wagon as they passed. The mountain trail had petered during the night (or else they'd taken a wrong turn in the dark), forcing them to reduce their speed on the heavily-forested descent. Upon reaching the lower foothills of the range, Doaks pointed them southward on the remains of another ancient highway of wide, crete lanes, claiming Gwenita's sensors had detected a functioning charge station. The land flattened quickly and, after a half hour of picking their way through a line of rusted autos, he took an exit for an old-world settlement called 'Carson City.'

This fallen metropolis stretched out in endless, mazelike avenues around the wagon as they hovered through, full of signs advertising places called 'casinos' that all claimed to have the 'loosest slots in town.' It was abandoned as far as they could tell, most of the streets covered in a thin layer of reddish-orange sand, with more of the stuff piled up in waist-high drifts against every vertical surface. And the farther east they went, the thicker the sand became. Soon it wasn't just coating the town, but *devouring* it. The roads were smothered and a few of the weathered buildings lay all but buried beneath massive dunes, blurring the line between desert and town. When they found the dilapidated ion charging station, it was one of the last manmade objects before the badlands took over entirely. Korden stood at the control deck and looked out at them as Doaks cozied the wagon up next to a pump.

This 'Valley of Bones' was *immense*. A flat ocean of cracked hardpan stretched as far as the eye could see, the uniformity broken only by hunched, sunbeaten sand knolls. In the distance, heat waves turned the ground into a squirming carpet. A stagnant wind fluttered out of that barren waste, carrying a bitter grit Korden could taste even with his mouth closed. The sky was a hazy, washed-out blue with only two objects in it: the blazing sun to the northeast, and the Shroud a few degrees south and a few sizes smaller. He'd never seen them both presented so starkly side-by-side like this, one eye-wateringly bright, the other a black hole in the sky, a study in extreme opposites. They made him think of the lessons Tash had taught him about the duality of human nature, and the emotions that would affect his artcraft.

The others had been sleeping inside the bonnet, but Korden heard them stir as the wagon settled on its fold-out support legs. After he untied Doaks from the control console, the phoney medicine merchant stood up for the first time in ten hours, his back popping audibly. He looked ridiculous wearing the canvas sack he'd been given in Ida's detention cells, especially with his stubby fingers studded in gaudy rings. Korden followed close behind as the man leapt down from the deck and walked stiff-legged around to the front of the vehicle.

"Oh Gwenita, sweetlove! What'd they do to yah?" He ran his hands along the dented front corner of the wagon where the last boulder had smashed into them, then cocked an eye at Korden. "So much for that magic, eh rubo?"

"I did what I could," Korden told him, not caring to elaborate about how Loathe had been eating his artcraft when he tried to deflect the giant rock. He wiped a sheen of sweat from his brow brought on by the heat. "How bad is the damage?"

"What do I look like, a mechaneer? How the hells should I know? It was drivin fine, but that don't mean half a million circuits and wires and…and…and *crystals* ain't all fried up inside!" He used one thumb to lovingly wipe away sand caked in several of the vehicle's seams. "I mean, yah gotta remember, this pretty lady is centuries old! And they don't make 'em like they used to. Which is to say, at all."

Korden sighed. No use worrying about what they couldn't change or predict. So instead, he asked, "How long until we can get on the move? I don't want to stay here too long."

"Yeah, if I had a whole posse of rotheads huntin me, I reckon I wouldn't either. C'mon, let's see how fast the ion is flowin." He beckoned with one finger as he stepped over and inserted the pump into the wagon. After watching the power gauge tick upward and performing some mental calculations, he declared, "Gonna be an hour to get her topped off, and prob'ly two fer each of the batteries."

"*Seven hours?*" Korden exclaimed. "We can't stay here that long, they could be coming for us right now!"

"Can't control the physics. She burned through a hellsuva lotta power with that run last night, and now we gotta replace it with this trickle. Either that, or risk her dyin out there on us 'fore we find another station. Don't worry so much though. We made some headway on 'em last night, and if we see 'em comin, we'll have to hightail it again and hope for the best." He shook his head and gave a mighty yawn. "Besides, Saint o' Christ forbid *I* get a little shuteye after drivin yah lazy asses around all night."

As much as Korden wanted to argue with the man—about everything that came out of his weaselly mouth—he was right. They needed to pace themselves, and not give in to panic.

IF IT EASES YOUR DISTRESS, SIR, I WOULD ALSO REMIND YOU THAT THE RUSH MIGHT NOT BE SO DIRE.

Stone made a good point. After Mayor Hildan revealed the box that the Prophet spoke through, the telepathic computer determined that he would be able to receive the broadcasts as well, plucking them out of these 'radiowaves' to play for Korden. According to Hildan, the cycle updated twice each day, every twelve hours, at precisely 3:30 A.M. and P.M., although Stone could find no significance for this particular time. When Korden had woken up this morning, the first new message (it seemed wrong to call it a *prophecy* or *prediction* when it dealt with events occurring in the present) informed him that the Incarnate detachment—and presumably Heater—was still centered around Ida in some kind of siege, just as Winstid had predicted in his dream. That made Korden feel terrible for the people there, but it also meant that the chase wasn't back on yet.

Korden watched Doaks setting up the pump for a few moments, then reached into the back pocket of his dungarees and drew out the map he'd been carrying since leaving the village. He held it out for the other man to see.

"By the Stranger's ash-black cloak, boy. Where'd yah get this?" Doaks whispered. His *mohol* lit up with awe as he accepted the map gingerly, as though afraid it would crumble to dust in his hands. "I know men'd give everything they own for a survey like this."

Korden tapped the tiny 'Carson City' label alongside Tay-ho. "This is where we are now. And this..." He slid his finger over to an X that Stone had directed him to mark, much farther to the right and a bit up, in the middle of a brown expanse of nothing where the single word 'Tuscarora' was written. "...is where we need to go next."

Doaks studied the mark while rubbing absently at his jaw, where the streak of gray meandered through his beard. "Way up there? Detour like that is sure gonna lengthen our trip."

"That's where the Prophet's signal is coming from."

"And I assume yah know that because 'magic?'"

Korden ignored the question. "I want to see if we can find him before we head on to the Skyreach. How long do you think it'll take to get there?"

"Gonna have to keep our speed down to conserve as much energy as possible. Stop at night to let Gwenita cool down. Even so, I'd say we should be able to hit it in…oh, two weeks and a bit. Maybe closer to three."

I CALCULATE A 92.5 PERCENT CHANCE THIS ESTIMATE IS GROSSLY INFLATED. IN A VEHICLE CAPABLE OF 70-MILE-PER-HOUR TRAVEL ON MAINTAINED ROADS, SUCH A TRIP WOULD LAST ONLY SIX HOURS. EVEN FACTORING IN THE WAGON'S MUCH LOWER MAXIMUM SPEED AND MR. DOAKS'S OTHER PARAMETERS, IT SHOULD TAKE NO LONGER THAN FOUR DAYS TO REACH OUR DESTINATION.

Korden summed up the detailed explanation in two words. "You're lying."

Doaks hiked an eyebrow, but there wasn't a trace of that devious quicksilver color in his aura as he said, "Hey, it might not look too far away as the creegan flies. Problem is, yah can't count on a straight route. Too many crevies out there, waitin to divert you off in a different direction for a hundred spans." He gave a noncommittal shrug. "Crossin the Valley of Bones means constantly backtrackin and sidesteppin. Takes patience and determination. Yah keep movin and hope yah luck holds."

Stone again expressed skepticism, but this time Korden said nothing. He folded the map back up and shoved it in his pocket while gazing out at that tract of searing orange sand.

"Are yah *sure* this is what yah want?" Doaks asked, in a far gentler tone than Korden had ever heard him use. "Cause it ain't gonna be a Seventh Eve party out there. Even if we don't run outta juice, I got no idea what that kinda heat'll do to Gwenita, or if the grit'll find its way into her engines. Then there's cactus scourge, suck sand, tweedle hawks, scorpigators…not to mention the sand spookies."

Korden smirked. "Sand spookies?"

"Yeah, sand spookies. Ghosts of the desert. Invisible beings livin under the sand. People been tellin stories about 'em for decades." He waved a hand. "Never your mind, don't matter. The point I'm tryin to make is, the desert is a hard place where a single mistake'll wipe yah out."

"It can't be that bad. You've crossed it before. And trade caravans do it all the time."

"No, they *attempt* it. Only two outta three make it. The rest just...disappear. Valley swallows 'em up. And the last time I got up the guff to cross it, nearly eighteen years ago, my team of mules died and I crawled the last twenty spans on my hands and knees. Spit up sand for a week. After that, I found Gwenita and kept myself to *this* side of the land." He propped an elbow on the sideboard of the wagon. "All I'm sayin is, it ain't too late to divert, maybe keep headin south into the Mex. Lotta ladies down there. Most of 'em are crones, but still..."

"I have to get to the Skyreach," Korden insisted. "One way or another."

"Fine. Suit yahself. But what happens to me when we get there?"

Korden gave him a questioning frown.

"What I mean is, what are yah offerin ta keep me at the helm?"

"Offering...? We broke you out of jail!"

Doaks flashed that broad, white-toothed grin which Korden had come to despise so much. "Yah only did that cause yah had no other choice. And I *let* yah do it cause I didn't either. But that's no basis for a healthy workin relationship."

Korden held up his arm, displaying the scabbed slashes below the bicep where this man had forced him to drain blood to sell in his stage show. "That's ironic coming from someone who treats their business partner like a milking cow."

The smile fell off the other man's face. "If I know the only thing waitin for me on the other side of that desert is another cell—or worse—what does that do for my morale? Better yet, how can yah trust that I'm not always gonna be lookin for a way ta roll over on yah? Havin a carrot to dangle is in *yah* best interest just as much as mine."

Korden sighed heavily. He hated to admit it, but Tarmon Doaks was a fantastic salesman. "All right. If you get us to the Prophet and then across the Valley of Bones, you can… go free," he said, each word as bitter as a mouthful of the sand around them. "I promise."

"And what about Gwenita?" Doaks prompted.

"You can have her. Not much good to me without you anyway." Before Doaks could react, Korden reached out, grabbed his wrist, held it against the side of the wagon, and sealed his hand there with artcraft-infused adhesive. "But you should be aware…if you *do* try anything before we get there…my magic can be used for a lot of horrible things."

Doaks's conniving grin resurfaced. "All right then. We have an accord." He tugged on his incapacitated arm. "I'd shake on it, but…"

Korden released him. As he walked away, the other man called out, "Oh, and do yah mind if I change clothes in the meantime? This canvas is beginnin ta chaff in some really uncomfortable places…"

2

As he made his way back along the wagon, the rear door retracted up into the bonnet and Lillam rushed out.

There had been no time to retrieve her belongings when they fled Ida, so she wore one of Rand's tunics like a shapeless dress that hung to her knees. Even though the garment swallowed her slender frame, the thick padding of makeshift bandages was still evident on her shoulder. She stumbled down the steps from the rear deck and ran a handful of paces away before falling to her knees and hunching over to void the soupy contents of her stomach onto the vermilion sand.

Rand exited next, hurrying after her. By the time he caught up, she was already standing. She gave him an irritated wave, muttered something about wanting to be alone, and walked away, her bare feet kicking up sprays of grit. The heat baking off the ground was so fierce, Korden didn't see how she could stand to touch it.

He approached Rand warily and asked, "Is she all right? Did the bullet make her do that…?"

The other man glanced at him, then went back to watching Lillam where she now stood with her back to them, farther up the waterless beach that lapped at the edge of the city. "It's not the shot. She's got the morning whimpers." At Korden's confused expression, he added, "The baby…it causes women to feel sick when they wake up."

"Oh." Korden frowned as Stone filled his head with medical minutiae that only left him more confused. "Why would it do that?"

"I don't know." The confession sounded both ashamed and helpless. Rand rubbed a hand across the bristles of his shaved scalp. "I don't know *anything* about babies. Or women either, as it turns out."

"She…she doesn't like me very much, does she?"

This time, Rand looked at him far more appraisingly. Judging by his *mohol*, he was trying to decide whether or not to lie about the answer to that question. "True," he admitted. "But right now she likes me even less, for dragging her into this 'monumental curseshow.' And I'm starting to think she might be right."

The conversation was cut short by a tuneless but cheerful whistling behind them. Meech emerged from the wagon with a frying pan and a sack full of eggs in his scarred arms. His color-spiraled tunic was gone, replaced by a grubby shirt the green color of lime, and a pair of dungarees patched with every type of fabric imaginable. He appeared better today; still pale and sickly, just not so jittery. "Who's hungry, drudes? Thought I'd cook up some breakfast and…" He trailed as he took in the merciless desert in front of them. "Oh fram, that doesn't look like a lotta fun, huh?"

"It's a desert," Rand said to his brother. "What did you expect it to look like?"

"I dunno. Never thought about it."

"Hm, you jumped into something without considering the consequences. Why does that not surprise me?"

"Maybe cause you're a framstick?"

Korden pointed at the pan in Meech's arms before the

bickering could escalate. "We should take stock of all the food before we eat any of it, to make sure our rations are small enough."

"Chill on drude, there's plenty! But I was thinkin, we might wanna gather some cordwood before we leave to cook it all, cause there prob'ly won't be a lotta stuff out there to burn."

Korden nodded even though he was fairly sure he could conjure something to meet their needs. Better prepared than contrite, as Fortholm used to say. "That's a good idea. After we eat, let's throw the junk out of the wagon to make room, then I'll gather some."

"I can do it," Meech blurted, his voice suddenly sharp. His aura strobed with a brilliant orange panic, yet he strove to keep his voice casual as he added, "What I mean is, we can split up and scrounge even more. Sound good?"

"Do we have time for all this?" Rand interrupted. "Shouldn't we keep moving?"

"Doaks says it's going to take seven hours to get the wagon and batteries fully charged. And besides, I can hear the Prophet's broadcasts now on this—" Korden held up the leather strap with Stone's casing, "—and the new announcement this morning said the Incarnates were back at Ida. I'll keep listening when it switches over this afternoon."

"Since you brought them up, let's talk about that." Rand's jaw clenched. "Those Incarnates used *shooters*. And rode on more hovering machines. Rotheads don't do that. They don't use human machines or technology at all."

Korden squirmed and closed his eyes. So much of the

previous night was a blur, lost in a flood of adrenaline and fear. "Something's changed."

"Or maybe they're just that desperate to get their hands on you. And what about the other guy riding with them? He sure as hells wasn't an Incarnate!"

The question slugged Korden deep in the stomach, momentarily forced the air from his weak lungs. He calmed himself before answering. "His name is Heater Kay. He used to be a really awful man, but now he's got a…a *presence* inside him. One far worse than any Incarnate."

Meech gave an exaggerated shiver as he set the pan and eggs on the wagon's rear deck. "That drude gave me serious creeps. His super loud voice…the way his fingers grew… And it's possible I coulda been, ya know, seein things, but did those bugs that stung us kinda look like him?"

Rand was watching Korden intently. "How did he do those things? What is he, another Crafter?"

Korden shook his head, disgusted by the comparison. "Absolutely not. I told you, artcraft works *within* the laws of the natural world. Its power is seeded in imagination, but it grows through truth. What he used was…" He thought of Loathe, the way the entity could only assume the forms of fictional people. How the Heater-bug briefly faded when he doubted its reality. He hadn't noticed until now, but even the welts had disappeared from their flesh at some point. "Lies. Fantasies from a diseased mind. And I think the more we see through the illusion, the less power they have."

"You yelled something about killing him," Rand pressed.

"I thought I did. But this thing inside him…it must have

brought him back. And it's dangerous. We have to keep away from him, at all costs. It can feed off us."

"*Feed?*"

"This won't be easy to understand, but this entity...eats imagination."

Rand shot his brother a skeptical glance. "What, like paintings and books? Filet of fiction with a side of water-color?"

"No, I mean right out of our heads. The very concept of imagination sustains this creature, our ability to create original thought. It can suck your mind clean, till there's nothing left."

"Guess Rand don't have much to worry about then," Meech said with a grin. "He ain't had an original thought since he became assistant mayor."

His brother frowned and shot him the small finger, before telling Korden, "Look kid, I've accepted a lot of strangeness since I met you without protect, but I need you to elaborate on that a bit more. What does that mean, 'till there's nothing left?' We won't be able to *imagine* anything ever again?"

"Well, uh, yeah. In the sense that your skull caves in and your brain gets liquified."

Both men stared at him, speechless.

"The same goes for my artcraft," he rushed to add. "When I used it around him, he...sort of...*absorbed* the magic before it could have any affect. And it made him stronger."

"That's great. Your powers are the whole reason I trusted you to get us to the Skyreach, and now you're saying they're useless." Rand threw up his hands and backed away from them, toward where Lillam waited. "If I'd been told that we'd have to deal with Incarnates on flying autos and a guy that caves in skulls, I might not've been so eager to book passage on this little pleasure cruise."

"Then feel free to jump ship at any time, man!" Meech shouted after him.

Rand turned away, but retorted over his shoulder, "Oh, go scavenge for your 'cordwood'! You're not fooling any-one with *that* crone's tale, little brother."

Meech's pale cheeks darkened, but he said nothing.

"You want to look for more of your drug, don't you?" Korden asked.

The other man sputtered a denial that his aura didn't support.

"You said you wanted to be rid of it. I thought that's why you came with me."

"I know, I do, I really do, but you don't understand what this is like!" Meech brought a fisted, shaking hand to his mouth and bit down on a knuckle. "The gimmies are *killin* me, drude! When I don't have anything, it's all I can think about! I don't wanna *actually* take it, I just need a tiny stash, an emergency prick, so I can know it's there, just in case!"

"No. There is no 'in case.' You can't have it around you. My *den-so* used to say that temptation is the slope that steepens the further down you go."

"Yeah, well, sounds like your '*den-so*' needs to get spun himself," Meech grumbled. He picked up the pan and eggs and set about digging a fire pit in the sand.

3

Which left only one of his fellow travelers to see about.

Zeega sat on the arched roof of the wagon, where she'd remained all night. Her dark, glistening face was aimed up at the sky in the direction of the Shroud when Korden came to stand beneath her. The reverent posture reminded him of the way Eddas used to sit shirtless in the sun to 'get his tan in order,' even though Feegran claimed such order often went hand-in-hand with something called 'skin cancer.'

"Hey," he called softly. "Are you all right?"

Perhaps she's undergoing some sort of hibernation or metamorphosis. If we get closer, there could be signs of—

"Hush, Stone."

On top of the bonnet, the riftling stirred at last, turning her amorphous head to look down at him. All five of her eyes were cloudy with some purplish fluid that could only be tears.

"What is it? What's wrong?"

"*Zeega is a traitor*," she moaned miserably, her gurgly voice choked with emotion. "She laid *versicrods* upon a master. Once word of this reaches the other broods, Zeega will be shunned. Barred from the homeland and denied the sweet silence. Hunted down by the masters and thrown into the fires of Magdenom, to be tortured for all eternity."

"Well...you saved *our* lives," Korden offered, wincing at how lame it sounded.

The gelatinous flesh around her mouth rippled back

in a hideous snarl, revealing clenched rows of needlelike teeth. "And why did Zeega do that? What keeps driving her to help this pathetic human? At first, she thought your claims were just confusing, but now Zeega suspects you used your foul *craeftus* magic to control her mind, like the other human did to you!"

Korden started to protest, but, judging from the way the riftling's sneer faltered, she must've read the truth for herself in his thoughts. Purple jets squirted from a couple of her eyes in tiny arcs, spattering the sand around his sneakers. "I'm sorry," he told her. "I know this is hard for you."

She clacked one of her foreclaws. "Zeega's feelings do not matter."

"Is that what the Incarnates told you?"

"Yes. A *hoshnitath's* only purpose is to serve the masters. Zeega has violated this, so her *yan* must now be extinguished. She invites you to perform the slaying."

"Wait on, do you mean…? No, I'm not going to kill you!"

"But this is beneficial for both parties. Zeega's life will end, and you will rid yourself of an enemy."

THE CREATURE MAKES AN INTERESTING POINT.

Several of the riftling's eyes rolled upward in a very human expression of irritation. "Thank you disembodied one. Zeega feels so much better having your approval."

Korden put his hands on his hips as he stared up at her. "You are *not* my enemy, Zeega. You're…my friend."

She hissed. "Zeega does not have 'friends'."

He sighed, then beckoned to her. "Can you please come down from there?"

The riftling hesitated, then used her squirming mass of

tentacles to slowly crawl down the back of the wagon until she sat on the rear deck, at eye level with him.

"You know what I think happened?" he asked. Her eyes narrowed in anticipation. "You started asking questions."

"Explain," she gurgled.

"My teacher—Tash—he used to have me do a mental exercise where he would present a topic, then make me ask all the questions about it that I could." Korden smiled as the memories surfaced. "He said that asking questions was the truest way to educate yourself. And that people who stopped asking them became ripe for subjugation. Do you understand what I mean?"

"Not in the least."

Korden took a moment to phrase his next attempt exactly as he thought Tash would've put it. "You never asked questions about the Incarnates before. You accepted everything they told you because that's how you were raised. But then you saw evidence of their lies for yourself, so it made you start asking. And all these things you've believed your whole life stopped making sense. That would confuse and frustrate anyone."

He expected another burst of fury from the riftling, but she sat contemplating, her eyes bouncing in all directions, before saying, "Be that as it may, Zeega still must decide what to do next."

"I understand, and I hope you decide that you don't have to die. But until you make up your mind, you're more than welcome to travel with us. All right?"

The riftling took a swift breath, as though preparing to speak, then her head made a brief spastic motion that he took for a nod. She turned and scuttled back up on top of the wagon.

4

The siege of Ida raged throughout the night, but the Incarnates accomplished little more than putting a few scratches on the fortress walls surrounding it. In all fairness, the attackers were too small a force to wage such a large-scale operation, too ill-equipped, and too hesitant to use the remaining shooter ammunition from the stores Heater had provided, but, dear Saint of Christ, the ineffectiveness made them look like the most pathetic wastelings to ever walk the allverse. When Heater arrived back at the settlement—as the first rays of morning flowed between the mountain ridges in a golden cascade—most of the demons cowered behind armored shields and horse carcasses, either to escape the rising sun or the constant stream of arrows being fired at them from the parapets.

"How you rotheads managed to get this far in your quest for universal domination, we'll never understand." Heater strolled up to the demon that seemed to be the current ranking officer, a Fearnaught named Goash that was standing outside the range of the arrows, in the shade of a small pine copse. "Hells' bells, man, that's a bunch of *farmers* in there. Farmers that are too scared to be in the same room with a woman."

Goash had the good sense to look chagrined about the situation. He was short but brawny, weighted down in armor with one of the canvas bodysuits favored by demons of the upper echelon beneath it, designed to protect their delicate skin from the sun. On his head sat a helm forged to resemble a bat folded over the crown of his skull. "We will keep them pinned 'til reinforcements arrive," he slavered. "Regent Torgas assured me the assembly call has gone out to every *Exatraedes* within his command. They trek this way even now, with all haste."

"Yeah, they do, but they ain't comin to help you bust open this sad little piñata." Heater cracked the knuckles of one leatherclad hand. "We're goin after the boy. The sooner the better. Rest of your kind'll link up with us as we ride. And then, once Bright is ours, we're gonna lead the Filament into battle against this 'Moambati' that you guys are so terrified of."

Goash bared his teeth. "I know what Torgas commands, but we cannot allow these mortals to—!"

Heater used Loathe's power to bring the steel bat on the demon's head to life. It squealed and sank its tiny metal fangs into Goash's scalp, tearing out a hunk of flesh whose underside was black with clotted blood. The Incarnate screeched and writhed and beat at his own head. Heater took a few moments to savor his pain and fear before releasing the creation from reality and seizing Goash by the shoulders.

"We got bigger problems than these framheads," Heater told him, pushing their faces so close that the brightness of the Incarnate's glowing irises made his eyes water. He didn't have time to deal with the constant we're-too-good-to-take-orders-from-you attitude that most of these assholes affected toward him. Loathe had been insistent that they continue the pursuit immediately, unwilling to let Bright gain any ground, but Heater persuaded the entity that the rational course of action would be to regroup with the Incarnates and use the resources at hand. Both he and Loathe were hungry—growing more so by the second—and the last thing Heater wanted was for his new partner to get antsy and start feeding on him. "The kid ain't alone anymore. He's built up a nice little entourage of scrappy humans and found himself a sweet ride that's takin him farther away from us each second. The little bastard thinks you won't follow him if he makes it all the way to the Skyreach. Curse, he's even got some black-and-purple octopus that single-handedly took out our last three trikes."

This got Goash's full attention. He paled—as much as Incarnates were *capable* of paling, anyway—and asked, "A riftling attacked you?"

"We don't know what you call it, but it looked like a lump of curse with a thousand tentacles and lobster claws stuck on it."

"And you're *positive* it was helping the Lightbringer?"

"It killed Bludgeen and another Incarnate, tore apart our engine, then leapt on the kid's wagon, right into his open arms. Any chummier and they'd be shoppin for engagement rings."

Goash frowned, considering this information, then nodded. "Yes. We will go after the Lightbringer. But the riftling must be destroyed as well."

"Whatever gets your putrid dick hard." Heater released the Fearnaught, satisfied. "But we're gonna need wheels. The kid is headin across the Valley of Bones next. We sure can't follow 'im into the desert on horseback."

"It will be difficult to find functioning human vehicles from the time before."

"Didn't say they need to function. Just find anything with four wheels, and we'll take care of the rest."

Goash's burning eyes narrowed as he regarded Heater. "Your magic is so powerful as that?"

"It will be once we get finished with this heap."

Heater left the Incarnate and strode toward the front gate of Ida. The archers on the parapet turned their arrows on him when he came within range, but he rendered them into a fictitious species of flying carnivorous weasels that turned back on their owners in a vicious cloud.

When he reached the portcullis, the guards on the other side had backed away and stood cowering halfway across the courtyard. Heater couldn't blame them; most of these men had watched him suck the brains out of their mayor's head a few hours before. He smoothed his waist-length beard and gave them his most winning smile through the iron crossbars.

"Listen up, sheepframmers," he announced, amplifying his voice. "We can tear a hole through this gate, come inside, and devour every last mind inside there. Or…you can open up voluntarily, let us take the hundred most creative souls this dungheap has to offer, and then you have our word the rest of you will be left in peace. Makes no difference to us, but it might to you."

There was a long pause while the men talked—and then argued—amongst themselves. A fight broke out. People were stabbed. Heater waited patiently through it all until the portcullis rose, as he knew it would.

"Let's go grocery shopping," he told Loathe, while the entity gibbered and raved with hunger inside his mind.

SUNK COST FALLACY

1

Except for Zeega, they all ate breakfast around a meager fire with the glaring sun beating down upon them in shimmering waves, hunched over their food to keep the sand from blowing into it. There was little conversation. Korden noticed that Lillam sat as far away from him as possible, holding her injured arm stiffly to her side as she leaned against Rand.

Afterward, he and Meech set about crating up the potions and jars and various paraphernalia in the wagon and stacking it all ouside, an undertaking that Doaks protested vigorously against.

"Yah promised I'd get the wagon back!" he howled.

"And you will," Korden confirmed. "But I never said anything about your fake curatives."

"What about all that scavenged technology though? That curse is priceless! *Priceless!* Yah can't just leave it in the desert to rot!"

"I'm not. We're going to burn it all before we leave."

Doaks's beady eyes bulged. "*Burn* it?"

Korden reached into one of the boxes and held up the electric prod and the mind-enslaving headband that had made him a prisoner in his own body. "I would never let anybody—especially *you*—get their hands on these. All of it gets burned except the talkies. We can still use those."

The first battery was finished charging by the time the shelves and cupboards had been cleared of everything but essentials. Korden left Doaks's care to Meech and enlisted Rand to help gather firewood from the collapsed structures closest to the wagon while he took his carry pouch and one of the talkies and foraged deeper into the ruins.

This Carson City was a lonely place, with a dry wind constantly moaning through the streets, but it was a sight to behold. For the next two hours, Korden lost himself amid the abandoned wonders of the old world. Everywhere he turned were fascinating new structures to explore— churches and grocery stores and the ever-present 'casinos'— but, with time weighing down, he limited himself to the ones that Stone said might be useful.

He'd found a small stash of canned food and a pair of slip- pered shoes in passing condition that might fit Lillam when Stone directed him into a structure labeled with the word 'PHARMACY'. The computer assured him this was the more reliable version of what Tarmon Doaks only pretended to be.

In the rubble of the store's front room, he found a 'first aid kit' with fresh bandages. The back half—where Stone said the most potent medicines were kept—had been thoroughly ransacked. While he sifted through more debris, Korden noticed a faded sign plastered to the glass wall separating the two parts of the store.

UNDER NEVADA EMERGENCY STATUTE 28C - 1.7a: ALL ABORTION-INDUCING DRUGS ARE AVAILABLE ON AN OVER-THE-COUNTER BASIS FOR ALL TRIMESTERS. PLEASE SEE A PHARMACIST FOR ASSISTED PREGNANCY TERMINATION.

Emotion crept up the back of his throat and lay on his tongue like bitter, rust-covered metal, a mixture of anger and disgust and sorrow. He thought of Winstid's story about his own child. Stone had explained to him that abortion was an important medical procedure and a sociological issue fought over since mankind's earliest days, all of which he understood. But committing such an act as a capitulation to the Filament seemed like a betrayal of the human race.

ACCORDING TO HISTORICAL RECORDS, FEW WOMEN TOOK ADVANTAGE OF THIS OPTION DURING THE PURGES.

"They were brave," Korden agreed. Then, while looking at the wreckage around him, he added, "But I guess it made little difference."

He continued wandering through the sand-covered streets, pretending that he was on a sightseeing tour in the old world. Pathomes lurked everywhere, sickly emotional fogs like the one he'd seen over Tay-ho and inside the power distribution center, colored in drab black and infected green and bile yellow. They surrounded entire buildings or filled their interiors to mark the places where terrible events had unfolded during the collapse of society. Where fear and anger had been experienced so strongly by so many people that they emotions had leeched into the very air and left a psychic stain. Korden steered well clear of them, but then he stepped through the shattered front door of a dim casino called 'Slots of Luck' and found a much smaller cloud that brought him to a standstill.

Unlike many of the establishments he'd entered, this one was mostly intact, with the gaming equipment in place. Surrounding a table in the middle of the casino floor was a pathome in a vibrant shade of scarlet.

Korden edged closer, curious but ready to run at the first sign of trouble. The fog was transparent enough that he could make out the table at its center, which had a low wall around the edges. The top was covered in a moldy green fabric with a complicated series of grids marked on it. Stone filled him on the rules of a game called 'craps' even as the pathome coalesced into the figures that had created the emotional echo.

A tight group of people made of brilliant red smoke cheered and clapped soundlessly as they gathered around a man at the far end of the table, who was shaking a fist and then making a motion as if tossing something across the fabric. Korden had seen the Olders playing dice back in the village often enough to recognize this part of the game. The man did this repeatedly, grinning wider each time, receiving claps on the back by those around him. Finally, one of the invisible rolls landed on something that caused him and everyone around him to raise their arms and scream in triumph. Korden heard their voices growing now, a jubilant cheer so infectious that he couldn't help smiling along with them.

In the emotional spectrum, reds were representative of the passions, that collection of feelings too urgent to be denied. But, while all the other pathomes he'd encountered thus far had been created from negative emotions, this hue was far lighter and more pleasant than the stark blood color of violence or danger. In fact, judging from the echoed spirits in front of him, he suspected it was a concentration of *excitement*.

Now that the scene from history had replayed itself, the figures noticed Korden for the first time. They drifted toward him, drawn to the living in order to share their emotion. The other *mohol* ghosts had sought to bog him down with their bitterness and fear and hatred, but these phantoms favored him with friendly, cheerful grins. Korden followed instinct and forced himself to stay motionless as they surrounded him. Their misty red arms reached to caress him.

Absolute elation spread throughout his body at their touch, an overpowering exhilaration that made him want to leap and dance and sing. He could see why this strong emotion had lingered long after its creators were gone. Korden closed his eyes and reveled in it, smiling dopily, wrapping his arms around himself in an ecstatic hug as he swayed slightly, until a creaking voice behind him asked, "Ya gonna need some privacy there, kid?"

2

He spun, the pathome receding now that its emotion had been shared, leaving him slightly cold and lightheaded. A wan lantern light shone through an opening at the back of the casino, flanked by rows of the 'slot machines' this city loved so much. Past the opening, he could make out the shapes of two people sitting on opposite sides of a table, watching him.

"I-I'm sorry!" Korden backpedaled. Experience had made him extremely leery of strangers. "I didn't know anyone was in here!"

"Ain't no skin off our noses," that scratchy voice answered. "Just makin sure ya wasn't about to strip and run around nekkid. This place's got that effect on people."

"Ya mean it's got that effect on *you*," a second, deeper-but-still-wheezy voice said, and both speakers cackled.

Korden kept an eye on them as he edged toward the door, but a second later he tripped over one of the slot machines toppled across the floor. He sprawled backward, knocking his rear end painfully against the filthy tile floor.

"Oh geezum, I'm sorry, kid." The first voice sounded contrite. "No need to run off. We ain't gonna bite. You're more'n welcome to sit in for a game or two if ya got the urge."

Korden got up and brushed himself off, then stood uncertainly. Stone was urging him to leave, but he got no sense of deceit or harmful intent from the auras in the other room. He walked back toward them, through the casino and the ranks of colorful slot machines covered in dust, and stopped in the opening to take in the scene on the other side.

The space beyond was nothing but a tiny alcove, with smaller fabric-covered tables scattered throughout that had been used for games called 'poker' and 'black jack' according to Stone, most of them now supporting oil lanterns that cast the room in a warm glow. Two bodlas sat at the table closest to the entrance, faces wizened and age-spotted, hands like knobby twigs. Both were as old as anyone he'd met in Hidden Glen, men in the final years of very long lives. They wore simple, open-throated tunics and baggy pantaloons; casual, comfortable clothing so washed and worn the colors had faded to a distant suggestion. Spread in front of them on the table was a deck of glossy playing cards with the 'Slots of Luck' logo on the backs, laid out in a configuration that Korden instantly recognized.

"Ya know how to play totala?" the man on the left, the one with the deeper voice, asked, noticing Korden's interest. He was tall and gaunt, with a huge, hawkish nose and utterly bald pate.

"Yeeesss," Korden answered carefully, striving to keep the excitement from his voice as he spoke the understatement.

The other man—shorter, with merry blue eyes and a ring of wispy white hair that began above his neckline and hung so low it brushed his shoulders—turned to his companion while pointing across his chest at Korden. "See there? *That's* what a good bluffin face looks like, ya serial folder."

"Mine was good enough to lift a week's wortha teabags off you yesterday."

Blue Eyes flapped a hand good-naturedly and shot Korden a grin that revealed a few teeth clinging to his shriveled gums. "What's the handle, kid?"

"Handle? Oh, uh, Korden."

"I'm Zigmund. The scarecrow over there is Telli."

"Nice to meet you," Korden said, wondering if it was.

"And how old are ya, Korden?"

"Sixteen."

"Ah, sixteen." Zigmund leaned back in his chair with a wistful grin. "What a horrible, horrible age. Ya c'n see the light at the enda the tunnel, but ya know ya prob'ly won't survive long enough to get there."

"So what brung ya out to the ass end of nowhere?" Telli asked.

"Just...passing through."

He lifted a bushy eyebrow. "Not out to the Valley, I hope."

"No. Up north," Korden lied.

"Good." Zigmund nodded his approval as he swept cards toward him. "Place'd eat ya alive. We been watchin it scour this city away a block at a time for the last two decades."

"You live here then?"

"Oh yeah, we each got our own suite right upstairs. Nuthin but the best for the last two residents of Carson City, Nevada." He brayed gasping, breathless laughter.

"It's just the two of you?" Korden asked. "In the whole settlement? Why don't you leave then?"

"Not much more out there than there is right here," Telli wheezed, lifting his narrow shoulders. "Least it's quiet, and we don't have to fight anyone over the scraps."

"And there's somethin about this place," Zigmund added, stopping mid-shuffle to gaze lovingly at the walls around them. "Makes ya happy just bein here. Like ya want to jump for joy all the time. Can't really explain it, but then, judgin by your swoon out there, ya already know."

They might not be able to explain it, but Korden could. These two men had been living in close proximity to the pathome in the main room for years. The emotional cloud would be invisible to them, but they could obviously sense the positivity it exuded. As Zigmund spoke of it, the same lively shade of red crept into his *mohol*. No wonder they didn't want to leave; this building was an oasis of happiness in otherwise dismal ruins. Even Korden felt the undeniable urge to run back and relive the sheer exuberance all over again. The 'joy fog' might even be the reason this casino was in such good shape compared to the others, had never been looted or wrecked.

"Enough jawin," Telli said. "If we're gonna play, let's play."

Zigmund set the cards aside. "Like I said, kid, you're welcome to sit in. Long as ya got somethin to ante, that is."

Korden frowned in confusion at the term and received an explanation from Stone and Telli simultaneously.

"We play for swag." The gaunt man lifted a sack from the floor beside him and set it on the edge of the table. "And we play for *keeps*."

Zigmund nodded and produced a sack of his own. "Every Second, Fourth, and Sixth Morn we go out scavengin, then play with whatever we find the rest of the week. Plenty of stash left in this city for the determined." He poked a finger at the carry pouch slung across Korden's chest. "Looks like ya found that out already, too."

Korden curled a protective arm around his pouch. "You mean...you bet?" He'd played totala for years with the Olders and gotten quite good at the game. It was played with multiple decks of cards, and additional packs added based on the number of players. The basic concept was similar to chess—infiltrating the enemy's castle—except that players hid their various pieces in personal and communal piles called 'towers'. The game was all about eliminating your opponents' high value markers while tricking them into attacking your worthless ones. Games could take hours, and there were many different goals and criteria a player could achieve, so there could be multiple winners. "But how does that work? What do you bet *on*?"

"We wager on findin each other's markers. If the guess is right, ya win. If it's wrong, ya lose. Never tried it with three people before, so it should be interestin."

"And no recycled bets," Telli added. "Once it's won, it's won. Only thing that's kept the game interestin for so long."

"I don't know," Korden said. "I should be going..."

Zigmund grabbed his wrist. "At least see what we brought to gamble with, in case somethin catches your eye!"

Both men stood hurriedly to dump their sacks out on the table. A cornucopia of various objects scattered across the fabric, matches and utensils and old-world clothing with writing that said things like, I LOST MY SHIRT IN CARSON! Korden saw nothing he couldn't live without.

Then Zigmund gave his bag a final shake, and two tiny, glittering cylinders hit the tabletop and rolled toward Korden.

Stone identified them before he could. THAT IS .45 CALIBER AMMUNITION, CAPABLE OF BEING FIRED BY YOUR FATHER'S PISTOL.

Korden picked up the brass tubes and held them in the palm of his hand. They were similar to the homemade bullets Clan Triker manufactured, but far sleeker and better-crafted; clearly products of the old world.

"Like those, do ya?" Zigmund asked, his aura pleased. "Found 'em in an old gun shop off Fairview. Place'd been ransacked, but those two little beauties rolled into a floor grate. 'Course, don't know what good they'd do without a shooter to put 'em in, but that's *your* business."

Korden didn't just like them. He *loved* them. He wanted more than anything to be able to load them into the empty weapon Redfen had given him for his sixteenth birthday months before. Not because he needed the gun, but because completing its existence would bring him a bit closer to the man who'd raised him.

"Tell ya what." Zigmund gave a sly, wrinkled grin. "Play a round, and I'll put 'em up as a pair."

"All right," Korden agreed. It would be a few hours yet before the batteries were charged. "Maybe just one game…"

3

He pulled a creaking, dust-covered chair over from another table, positioned it between them, and eased into it while asking, "Aren't you worried about Incarnates catching you with me?"

"I'm seventy-eight frammin years old, my eyesight's goin, and my back hurts every damn second of the day," Telli muttered. "If those black-blooded bodyhoppers don't have anything better to do than hunt *me* down, I feel sorry for 'em."

"Still," Korden persisted, "there are a lot of them after me, and they'll be coming this way soon."

"Unless you're plannin on movin in, I don't think we'll have a problem."

"Now, pay attention," Zigmund chided, all seriousness as he dealt out the player hands and communal towers. "We'll give you the rundown on how to wager."

They coached him on how to set up an ante line, with a progressive order of bets you were offering. Korden brought items out of his bag that he could bare to part with, even though he was sure it wouldn't be an issue; he was such a mean totala player that several of the Olders had refused to partake in games with him. Both men were interested in the canned goods he'd scavenged, several of the books he'd brought from the village, and assorted other odds and ends he had on him. He arranged them all beside him in order of least to most importance. Zigmund placed the two bullets midway down his own ante line, which would force Korden to go through the other wagers to get to them.

They raised their banners, built their personal towers, hid their markers among them, and were ready to begin. By luck of the draw, Zigmund opened, and the beginning rounds consisted of cautious moves as they disseminated their cards throughout the various towers where they believed them least likely to be found.

It was Telli that drew first blood, revealing his red Brute in order to flip the top three cards of Korden's left tower, where his black Tipper was hiding.

"I believe *that's* mine, thank ya very much," he croaked, reaching to take the can of corn at the front of Korden's ante line.

"But...why would you do that?" Korden asked. "You took such a big chance in leaving your Brute exposed and gained almost nothing. If I take it on my next turn, you'll never bust the Dragon Gate."

"Not interested in bustin gates." Telli winked as he shook the can, sloshing the contents. "I just want the swag, kid."

As the game progressed, Korden's bafflement only grew. These men weren't playing to storm the ramparts or run up their bounties; they merely made plays that allowed them to win offerings from the other players. It was a completely different approach to the game, one that was antithetical to all traditional strategies. By the time Korden started adapting his playing style, he'd lost most of his wagers, yet was no closer to the winning the coveted bullets.

"There's your Ramble Knight." Zigmund flipped over the last of Korden's central tower. The discovery of the marker had a bounceback effect that wiped out the bodla's defenses, yet he seemed ecstatic as he slid the worn copy of *The Old Man and the Sea* from Korden's ante line to his own side of the table. The book had been given to him by Skewtz years ago, and seeing it leave his possession sent a pang of regret through Korden's heart.

"Looks like it's curtains for you, kid," Telli told him with a phlegmy chuckle.

"But I'm winning by every measure!" Korden complained.

"At the game, maybe. But your bets are gettin miiighty thin."

Korden gritted his teeth in frustration. He had two

items left, but the only spoils he'd won so far was when one of them guessed incorrectly and forfeited a wager from their lines. Telli had won so much from Zigmund that the coppery bullets were next up for the taking, but Korden needed a way to ensure he got them.

The Olders taught him never to read auras while playing games such as this, but it didn't matter anyway. Like all the best totala opponents, these two men kept their emotions as carefully in check as their faces; their *mohols* were blank, gray slates as they played. Out of sheer desperation, Korden asked Stone if there was anything the computer could do to help.

I *COULD* CUT DOWN YOUR MARGIN OF ERROR CONSID-ERABLY BY ANALYZING CARD COUNTS AND CROSS-REF-ERENCING THEM WITH YOUR OPPONENT'S PLAY STRATE-GIES…BUT ASSISTING WITH SUCH CHEATING IN A GAME OF CHANCE VIOLATES MY DECENCY PROTOCOLS.

Wait on, Korden thought back. *You mean the one time I NEED you to calculate odds, you won't do it?*

FRANKLY, SIR, I THINK YOU SHOULD BE ASHAMED OF YOURSELF FOR EVEN ASKING.

Another three rounds went by and, despite the fact Korden had just about wiped out both men on the field of battle, his gambling went bust.

"Well, that's it, my friend." Zigmund reached over to pat his hand reassuringly. "This game ain't for everybody."

"Please, I *need* those bullets." Korden dug through his carry pouch, past Redfen's shooter and the rest of his belongings, looking for something else they might be interested in.

SIR, I REALLY THINK YOU SHOULD CONSIDER STOPPING.

But I've already lost so much, I can't walk away!

YOU AND I MUST HAVE A LESSON ON SUNK COST FALLACY
WHEN THIS IS OVER.

At the very bottom of his carry pouch, Korden's fingers touched a slick, rectangular box that he couldn't identify. He pulled it out and heard Zigmund give a strangled cry of excitement.

In Korden's hand was one of the small boxes he'd taken from the back of the rusted cargo wagon outside the village, the ones in a clear wrapper with the word 'Kool' printed on them. Zigmund held out a shaking hand. Korden put the box in it. The bodla held them under his nose and inhaled deeply.

"Aged be damned, they're *sealed*," he whispered. "I ain't had tobaccy in years, let alone some fine-rolled 'rettes from the old world!"

"I've got more of them!" Korden drew out the other two packs and laid them on the table. "I'll give them all to you in exchange for both bullets!"

Zigmund licked his spotted lips as he considered, but Telli slapped the table in protest. "Now, wait on a tick, Zig! This ain't no tradin post! Ya know the rule: we gamble and win, or we walk away disappointed! That's what keeps the feel-good magic happenin in here!"

The other man nodded in agreement and thrust the package of 'rettes back at Korden. "He's right. I gotta win 'em, fair and square."

Korden scowled and considered telling them the truth about their 'feel-good magic,' but it would probably just turn them against him. "Then deal again."

It took them a few minutes to get a new game set up. Zigmund took the opportunity to redistribute his ante line, moving the bullets down in the rankings. This time, Korden threw out all the totala strategy he'd ever learned and concentrated on playing the game like them: recklessly, and with a complete disregard for sensible rules. He began attacking at the first opportunity and found several of Zigmund's markers, enough to move the cylinders back up the line.

But it was Telli that made advances on Korden, taking the first two packs of 'rettes for himself. Sweat beaded Korden's forehead as he realized he was almost out of chances. Zigmund looked just as distressed himself, seeing his opportunity slip away. He undertook a series of random attacks on Korden's towers, but each one found nothing and lost him wager after wager until the bullets rose to the top of his ante line.

Korden pulled back this time, denying the urge to attack, and let the other man come to him.

"There!" Zigmund proclaimed, using his Leper to infect Korden's last tower. "That's the last place your Floral Queen could be."

Korden flipped the decimated pile over, revealing nothing but low cards.

"*Nooo!*" the old man howled, tossing his cards on the table. "*That's impossible, where else could she be?*"

Korden lowered his playing hand to reveal the marker.

"But...b-but...no one keeps her in their hand," Zigmund whispered. "That's the dumbest thing you could do."

"Only if you're actually playing the game," Korden said.

Telli chuckled. "I'll have to remember that one, kid."

"Thanks for the game." Korden took the bullets, dropped them into his bag, and made to clear off the rest of his meager ante, but Zigmund clasped his spindly hands on the table in pleading.

"Ya gotta give me a chance to win that last pack, ya just gotta!"

Korden considered. "Put up a few of those extra totala decks and it's a deal."

4

He said his goodbyes and made it back outside to the street before stopping to pull out the pistol and bullets. With Stone's guidance, he made sure the safety was activated, ejected the 'magazine', loaded the shots, and snapped it back into place.

The gun felt different in his hands now. Alive, somehow. As dangerous as a coiled snake, with the trigger as its fang. He held it in front of him, aimed down the barrel, and tried to imagine shooting someone on the other end. The fantasy brought a shiver of revulsion. He'd seen the devastation that such shooters wrought, and it wasn't something he would ever wish to inflict on another human being. There was something messy and...and *undignified* about battling your enemy by poking holes in their body and letting the blood spill out. Besides, he considered his artcraft a far more effective weapon than this hunk of metal could ever be.

Nevertheless, it was a tool Redfen wanted him to have, and he would keep it safe in case he needed it.

Stone broke into his contemplation of the newly loaded pistol.

SIR, THE PROPHET'S AFTERNOON BROADCAST HAS GONE LIVE. I THINK YOU NEED TO HEAR IT IMMEDIATELY. He didn't wait for permission before unleashing that upbeat voice in Korden's head, the one he'd first heard in Mayor Hildan's office.

Woooah there pussycats, this is the Weatherman and I've got a lot *to report today! First off, the Incarnates that took over Lake Tahoe put the squeeze on one of the settlements there in a truly bizarre skirmish; there appears to be casualties, but I'm not sure how. After the citizens let them inside the walls, whole swaths of people just sorta... went belly up, all at the same time.*

"Loathe," Korden whispered.

Now they're on the move again in a fleet of vehicles, heading east toward Carson City, and they are not *alone! The initial group looks to have grown to a hundred demons, maybe one-fifty, with more joining up all the time. Not only that, but I'm seeing movement up north from Washington to Montana and down south all along the border as even more regiments roll toward the Great Basin Desert! This has got to be the largest coordinated Incarnate effort I've seen on the western half of the country in a century or more! I don't know what set the bees to buzzing—or if it has anything to do with that chase last night and the vehicle that blasted out of Tahoe—but the Weatherman will keep you updated!*

"He knows about us!" Korden exclaimed. "And he's lived more than a century! He *must* be a Crafter!"

IT IS THE CONTENT OF HIS MESSAGE THAT MOST CON-
CERNS ME. IF HIS INFORMATION IS ACCURATE, IT SOUNDS
AS THOUGH THE INCARNATES ARE GOING TO CONSIDERABLE
LENGTHS TO APPREHEND US.

"One hundred and fifty," Korden murmured. More than he could possibly fight even if Heater wasn't leading them.

And they were heading this way right now.

"We'd better get back to the others."

5

Following Stone's directions, he arrived back at the fueling station a half hour later.

But he could hear angry, shouting voices echoing through the dead streets from several blocks away.

Korden sprinted toward his new companions and arrived panting at the wagon to find Rand holding Doaks against the sideboard. He was shouting in the smaller man's face while Meech and Lillam stood nearby.

"You're a framming liar and I won't let you get away with it!" Rand bellowed.

"Sorry yah feel that way, rubo." Doaks tilted his head and shrugged as though unconcerned by the violence being directed at him. He'd changed out of his burlap jumpsuit into the britches and ruffled shirt from one of his snazzy stage outfits. "But maybe yah should talk ta the kid before yah do anything rash. This is *his* show, ain't it?"

Meech caught sight of Korden and ran to meet him. "Drude, I'm so sorry, I shoulda told you first, but I kinda forgot all about it until a few minutes ago!"

"Told me what?"

"That this piece of curse *lied*." Rand poked a finger into Doaks's hefty chest. "The wagon isn't loyal to him at all. There's just a trick to starting it, and Meech has got the lay of it. We don't need this charlatan at all."

"That's not true!" Doaks strained to look at Korden around Rand. "Sure, maybe I tweaked the truth a bit to save my own skin, but yah still need me! Who knows this vehicle better than I do? And have any of *yah* ever crossed this hard, dried-up barren?"

"He's right," Korden said. "We made a deal."

"And I'll honor it, I swear!"

"Fram your deal," Rand snapped. "This man *cannot* be trusted. He's a liability. A danger to all of us. And I'm not willing to risk Lillam and the baby's lives having him around."

"If you intend to come with us, that's not your choice." Korden still wasn't comfortable commanding this expedition, but if they were going to keep thrusting the role on him, he might as well use it. "We need him."

"Then if you won't listen to reason…" Rand let go of Doaks, turned to the crates on the ground, and snatched up the silvery headband. "Give us a little peace of mind."

A knot of pure resolve hardened in Korden's chest. He scowled. "I told you, that's never going to be used on another person again."

"But *WHY*?" Rand gripped the metal band in both hands hard enough to whiten his knuckles. "Why are you always climbing onto some moral high ground when the rest of the world is content to roll in the dirt? Well, I guess it's up to me to do what you don't have the stomach for!"

He walked toward Doaks with the band as the other man cringed away.

Korden's will flickered out. This time, he was careful to control it, to keep his emotions in check lest the raging river inside him be set free to act on behalf of his impulses and underlying desires. The metal crumpled and then shattered in Rand's hands, spilling colored wires and strange, technologic innards onto the sand at his feet.

Rand stared down at the pieces for an unbearably long time, his aura simmering, then said quietly, "In case you're not aware…you're no hero. You're just a kid with a lot of ignorant ideas. And sooner or later, you're going to realize it. I hope it happens before you get us all killed."

He dropped the twisted remains of the headband and walked away. Lillam shot Korden a smug look and then hurried after him.

"Thanks," Doaks began. "That guy's a real—"

"Unhook the batteries and get us moving," Korden ordered. "The Incarnates are on their way."

Doaks seemed to sense that he'd reached the end of his goodwill. "Will do, Cap'n." He hustled toward the ion pumps on the far side of the wagon.

Meech watched him with his sunken, bruised eyes. Korden swept a hand over Doaks's treasures and told him, "The rest of this must be burned to ash before we leave."

The other man nodded, picked up a crate, and walked toward the fire.

Korden stood where he was, breathing slow and deep to subdue the angry inferno inside him.

He was still fuming when Stone said tentatively, MY

APOLOGIES, SIR, BUT COULD YOU DIRECT YOUR ATTEN-
TION BACK TO THE HEADBAND? THE INTERIOR PIECES, IN
PARTICULAR. I NOTICED SOMETHING THAT MIGHT BE OF
INTEREST.

Korden squatted on the sand and sifted through the shattered remnants until he found the fragment Stone meant.

Amid the greenish squares and wire snippets that made
up the band's innards was a silvery plate engraved with
three words:

MOAMBATI INDUSTRIES, INC.

CREVIES AND COLLABORATIONS

1

The Valley of Bones consumed them for the next three days.

Korden had read much about deserts and the harshness they contained, but none of it prepared him for the reality, neither physically nor mentally.

He didn't see how anyone could navigate such featureless wastes without computers like Stone or Gwenita. Everywhere he looked was the same vast, unbroken, orange plain, with only the sand dunes or an occasional cactus to measure their movement against. Most of the time, even the sun and Shroud remained hidden behind a yellowish haze in the air, suspending the wagon in a strange, bright void. The emptiness confused the mind and defied the eye.

And Upper have mercy, the heat! It was brutal even in the shade, but direct sunlight possessed an actual, physical *weight*, as though trying to smash you flat before it scorched you. Doaks shut down as many of Gwenita's secondary systems as possible to preserve their precious energy, which included something called 'climate control' for the bonnet.

As a result, the temperature inside the cramped quarters soon became unbearable. They opened both doors to let the dry wind blow through as they rode, but it did little except evaporate the constant sweat that poured from them and allow sand to accrue in every crease and corner. With their water supply tightly rationed, Korden's throat throbbed uncomfortably by the end of each day, and his tongue felt like a dead, dried-up slug inside his mouth. At least his lungs enjoyed the arid conditions; he couldn't remember ever being able to breathe this easy.

Then, as if in cruel jest, the temperature plummeted after the sun went down, resulting in nights chilly enough to bring on shivers. Korden didn't see how any land could be capable of such diametric extremes.

But they made progress, even at the snail's pace they were limited to. Stone kept him updated on the spans they crossed, which accumulated rapidly. Korden would've been willing to take turns at the controls so they could push straight through, but Doaks insisted they stop each night, not only to let Gwenita cool down, but because using her headlamps in the dark would be yet another power drain. The lost time made Korden anxious, but their nightly encampments gave them a chance to get some distance from one another.

Because they did little speaking or interacting, despite being crammed inside the same tiny room for twelve hours a day. Doaks stayed at the controls, of course, while Rand and Lillam mostly kept to themselves in their curtained corner of the bonnet, the woman giving Korden scowls whenever their paths crossed. Even the pair of shoes he'd scavenged for her did little to change her contempt. Korden used the opportunity to faith and write, activities that he'd mostly neglected since leaving the redwood forest. Hopefully, the renewed lessons in concentration would lend him a little more control over his rampaging artcraft. He passed the rest of the time playing endless rounds of totala with Meech, who picked up some healthy color to his skin, though his hands shook when a fit of his *gimmies*—what Stone called 'withdrawals'—came on.

Each morning, Korden expected to find Zeega gone, slunk off into the desert to die or perhaps back to her masters to beg their forgiveness. But the riftling remained perched on the roof like a gargoyle, coming down only to accept her portion of water and the evening meal, which she grudgingly ate.

The broadcasts from the Prophet continued as well, every twelve hours, as dependable as the sun. Each one painted a grimmer picture that Korden had yet to share with the others: the Incarnate legion at their back—swollen to more than 200 in number—was slowly gaining on them, with hundreds more racing toward them from the farthest reaches of the land.

2

I STAND CORRECTED. UPDATING MY INTERNAL FILES NOW...

It was the morning of their third day in the Valley, less than an hour after they'd set out. Korden and Doaks stood on the precipice of a deep cleft in the earth, a yawning chasm fifty pargs wide that slashed across the desert floor from northwest to southeast. Even with Doaks's farviewers, they could see no end to the ravine in either direction, as though it were designed specifically to cut them off and force them to turn back. It wasn't too deep—the bottom couldn't be more than three times Korden's height—but the walls were strangely sheer and as smooth as glass, not at all what one would expect from nature.

"What'd I tell yah: crevies." Doaks hawked a wad of phlegm into the trench as though reprimanding its existence. "Valley's rotten with 'em. Surprised we ain't hit any before now. They twist and meander and corkscrew around like a maze. People've tried to map 'em, but they seem to rearrange every time yah look away."

THIS 'CREVY' ALSO APPEARS TO BE A SPLIT IN THE LOOSE SAND ITSELF, RATHER THAN A WEATHERING THROUGH ROCK STRATA. SUCH GEOLOGIC FEATURES ARE CONTRARY TO PHYSICS, LET ALONE THE TERRAIN OF THE GREAT BASIN DESERT, BUT—

A lot could've changed since your last M-Net update, Korden finished for him, wiping sweat from his brow. Even this early, the heat was bad, but, in another hour, direct sunlight would be all but impossible to stand in. It gave him some insight as to how Incarnates must feel.

Which wasn't really a perspective he wanted.

The others emerged from the bonnet to see what had caused the halt. Rand and Meech hopped off the deck and walked toward them. Even Zeega climbed down from her perch. As she scuttled along beside them, Meech turned to the riftling and made an attempt at conversation. "So, um, aren't you…ya know…hot? Riding up there in the sun all day?"

"The *hoshnitath* heat tolerance is much higher than a human's. The wind of our passage is sufficient to keep Zeega cool." Her voice lowered to a harsh, gargled growl. "Even were it not so, death would be preferable to confinement inside that craft."

"Oh, yeah. I forgot, Doaks kept you prisoner too, huh?"

"Indeed. And one day, Zeega would very much like to repay the bloated human for his many mercies during their time together." She fixed the aforementioned bloated human in a withering stare with all five of her eyes, opened her foreclaws, and snapped them shut with a menacing *crack!*

Meech shied away from her with a shaky grin. "Well, that's kye, I guess. Um, give a shout if you need anything up there."

"Your concern is unnecessary, polluted human," she told him, before wandering over behind a stand of cacti, presumably to relieve herself.

"What's the hold up?" Rand demanded as they reached Korden and Doaks. It was the first words Korden had heard him say since their fight on the outskirts of Carson City. Rand gestured at the crevy. "Can't the wagon get us across that?"

Doaks shot him an annoyed look. "She *hovers*, she don't fly. Try to float over that and even if we don't smash to pieces at the bottom, we'll be stuck down there. Yet another reason why we shouldn't drive in the dark. So, unless our young Cap'n here has a magical way to get us to the other side..."

"Hey, yeah, this sure seems like an adjective situation to me," Rand added.

Korden shook his head. This chasm was far wider than the one he'd sailed over in the Sierras. And that situation had also just been him, not a wagon full of people, and he'd still needed a catalyst in his makeshift catapult. "There's a physical cost to using artcraft like that. It requires extreme willpower and concentration. Something as heavy as the wagon would be…taxing."

"You can't…conjure a bridge, or something?"

"There would be dangers in that as well. I don't know anything about bridge-building; what if I didn't create one that was strong enough, or the sand on either side didn't support it? I could try, but it wouldn't be worth the risk if we can find another way."

Rand snorted and muttered something unintelligible, his *mohol* steeped in frustration.

Doaks blew air between his teeth. "Then we gotta pick a direction. There's no tellin how far this crevy sprawls or if either end runs into another one, but goin south would—"

"Actually, we stand a 15.8 percent chance of shortening our distance by going north," Korden interrupted.

They all turned to him.

"So…yah also a human abacus?" Doaks asked skeptically.

Korden sighed. Perhaps explanations would be easier if he got this over with. "Stone, make them all registered users."

REQUEST COMPLETED, ALTHOUGH THIS COULD SLOW COMPUTATIONAL CYCLES SIGNIFICANTLY.

All three men jumped like their rear ends had been paddled and searched the empty desert around them for the speaker.

"His name is Stone, he's a telepathic computer, don't ask questions." Korden lifted the leather strap around his neck as an introduction. "According to his calculations, north is the way to go."

CORRECT, EVEN ACCOUNTING FOR POSSIBLE BACK-TRACKING.

"It's in my *brain*," Meech moaned, putting his hands to his temples and squashing his face. "I don't know if I can handle that, man."

"Amazin. To think that little wonder was under my nose the whole time." Doaks grinned wistfully, his gaze greedy as he took in the computer's shell. "Anyway, as I was *goin* to say, Gwenita picked up another functional ion station somewhere to the south. If we can pick our way to it and top off before we turn north, might be worth the detour."

REVISING CALCULATION... INDEED, IF SUCH IS THE CASE, SOUTH WOULD BE A BETTER OPTION.

"Great," Rand grumbled. "Now we're taking orders from a rock."

They all returned to Gwenita, but Korden followed Doaks onto the control deck, which they'd shaded by affixing wood to the front of the bonnet, then draping cloth overhead to create an awning. He waited while the man kicked on the engines, pointed them south, and drove along the edge of the crevy. Korden had been steeling himself to have this conversation for days, but couldn't put it off any longer.

"I need to know where you got that headband."

Doaks laid his forehead on his palm. "Oh, fer...! Let it go, boy. It's gone, yah broke it. It can never hurt yah again."

"That's not why I'm asking." He swallowed. "When I broke it open…there was a label inside that said, 'Moambati Industries.' Were you aware of that?"

The man raised his head to study Korden. His aura registered legitimate surprise as he asked, "It did? No, I had no idea. But surely yah don't think…?"

"How did you get it?" Korden reiterated. The last thing he wanted was to share his theories with this man.

"Same way I got Gwenita: scavengin in one of the city wastes. I'm talkin about the *big* cities now, those old-world megalopoles full of glittering towers and endless crete, so large yah could get lost and never find yah way out. The sea had crept up in this one, so most of it was flooded out. If I remember right, the folks livin 'round the outskirts called it 'Newer Leans.' On account of the buildings all leanin, I guess." He frowned at the memories. "Found it in this 'scraper fulla weird old tech. Had no clue what it was for. Kept it on a shelf for years before I tried it out on a dog of mine. Got that mutt to stand on his hind legs and dance a jig on stage. Other than that, I couldn't figure a way to use it for much. Until yah came along, that is."

"Glad I could help." Korden had to force his hands to unclench after hearing the man's cavalier tone. "Then what do you know about Moambati?"

"Same rumors as everybody else, I s'pose. Some kinda presence in the mountains of the Skyreach. Travel beyond has been cut off. Incarnates won't go near there anymore, which has got some of those dumb yokels brave enough to breed."

"What about entire towns disappearing?"

Doaks rubbed his beard and nodded slowly. "Heard that, too. Can't say as there's any truth, but I ain't been to the other side of the Valley in years." His eyes narrowed. "What *is* your plan here, boy? Why're you so intent on truckin east, anyway?"

"Just...get us there," Korden told him, and retreated into the wagon.

3

RECORDS ON TERESE MOAMBATI'S EARLY CHILDHOOD IN HAITI ARE NON-EXISTENT, BUT IT IS KNOWN THAT SHE EMIGRATED TO THE UNITED STATES AT THE AGE OF 19 IN 2095, Stone said. HOWEVER, THERE ARE RUMORS THAT SHE SERVED AS SOME SORT OF VOODOO PRIESTESS IN HER HOMELAND.

"What's 'voodoo'?" Korden asked as he squirmed on his bedroll, trying to even out the lumps in the cooling sand beneath him. The frigid air turned his words into an icy plume.

The computer had needed only a few hours to 'background compile' information on Moambati Industries, but Korden made him wait until they'd stopped for the night so he could concentrate on the findings. Now he lay beneath the wagon's rear deck as darkness swept across the vast desert, hoping the cover would keep sand out of his mouth while he slept. The others had scattered across the gently sloping dunes to sleep in makeshift tents after another admonishment from Doaks to watch out for the pits of loose grit called 'suck sand.' It was so cold tonight that they'd all taken extra blankets to bed with them.

Stone answered his question while pumping the necessary points of reference into his head. VOODOO IS A RELIGION WITH ROOTS IN AFRICAN CULTURE; HOWEVER, SOME LATER-GENERATION SECTS—AND MUCH OF POPULAR CULTURE—ASSOCIATE IT WITH MAGICAL RITUALS AND PRACTICES.

"Magic? Like artcraft?"

AS MUCH AS IT PAINS ME TO ADMIT, THE RESULTS OF SUCH SORCERY WERE PROBABLY FAR LESS QUANTIFIABLE THAN YOURS, SIR. MUCH OF VOODOO RITUAL IS CONCERNED WITH RAISING THE DEAD TO LIFE.

Korden gnawed the inside of his cheek as he considered this. "All right, go on."

AFTER EMIGRATION, MISS MOAMBATI LIVED WITH RELATIVES WHILE SHE ATTENDED THE PRESTIGIOUS LOUISIANA TECHNICAL AND ENGINEERING COLLEGE IN NEW ORLEANS ON MULTIPLE SCHOLARSHIPS.

"Newer Leans!" Korden exclaimed. "That's where Doaks said he found the headband!"

IT DOES STAND TO REASON. ALTHOUGH THE QUESTION ISN'T WHETHER THE HEADBAND IS CONNECTED TO THE COMPANY, BUT RATHER IF THE COMPANY IS CONNECTED TO THE ENTITY OF THE SAME NAME CURRENTLY LURKING WITHIN THE SKYREACH.

"You're just mad I figured it out before you could tell me."

I'VE ALWAYS CONSIDERED OUR WORK COLLABORATION, the computer bristled. AS I WAS SAYING, PERSONAL ACCOUNTS DESCRIBE HER AS SHREWD BUT DRIVEN, WITH LITTLE PATIENCE FOR ANYONE SHE SAW AS A HINDRANCE TO HER RESEARCH. HER EXCELLENT GRADES, LAB WORK, AND INTERNSHIPS QUICKLY MARKED HER AS A NEAR-GENIUS INTELLECT AND HAD MULTIPLE CORPORATIONS SEEKING TO

EMPLOY HER. I HAVE A PHOTO IF YOU WOULD LIKE ME TO REVEAL IT TO YOUR CONSCIOUS MIND.

He granted permission, and a picture appeared in Korden's mind of a very dark-skinned woman wearing a mannish tunic and pants, her black hair pulled into a frazzled tail on the back of her head. The foto appeared to've been taken without her knowledge as she entered the glass doors of an old-world building. Her mouth was set in a firm scowl below hard eyes that glinted with intensity.

WITH THE HELP OF SEVERAL INVESTORS, SHE FOUNDED HER OWN COMPANY IN 2101. BRAINWARE RESEARCH GROUP GARNERED MULTIPLE PATENTS ON MEDICAL DEVICES WHICH REVOLUTIONIZED THE HEALTHCARE INDUSTRY, FOCUSING MAINLY ON MAPPING, UNDERSTANDING, AND TREATING THE HUMAN BRAIN. MOST OF THE RESEARCH WAS SO ADVANCED, OTHER EXPERTS IN THE FIELD HAD TROUBLE COMPREHENDING IT. ONE PROMINENT FIGURE ACCUSED HER OF 'TECHNOLOGICAL WIZARDRY.'

"Another accusation of magic," Korden whispered. "But how can technology be magic? Tash always said they stood at odds with one another."

AS I HAVE STATED PREVIOUSLY, IT IS A COMMON HIS-TORICAL THEME FOR HUMANITY TO VIEW ADVANCEMENTS IN SCIENCE AS SUPERNATURAL. HOWEVER, IN THIS CASE, I AM 94.3 PERCENT CERTAIN THE COMMENT WAS SARCASTIC.

"Your human brain will be stunted."

Korden jumped as Zeega's head appeared over the edge of the deck above him. "What do you mean?"

"It will make you lazy to have information inserted into your mind in such a manner."

I BEG YOUR PARDON, BUT ALL LAWSUITS ALLEGING SUCH CLAIMS WERE DISMISSED FOR LACK OF EVIDENCE! NOW, IF YOU DO NOT MIND, YOU ARE EAVESDROPPING ON A PRIVATE CONVERSATION.

"No, it's all right," Korden said. "It might help to hear her thoughts."

The riftling rubbed two tentacles together as she settled on what passed for her haunches. "This woman indeed sounds like another *craeftus* to Zeega."

"If so, she would've been around before...before the others started appearing." He'd stopped short of saying 'before the Filament invaded.' Which was a pointless omission, considering the two other participants in the conversation could both read his mind.

THAT IS CORRECT, BUT I AM AFRAID THIS NEXT PART WILL ONLY ADD FURTHER CREDENCE TO SUCH A THEORY, Stone told them. BECAUSE, FOR THE NEXT 15 YEARS, BRG GREW IN SIZE, REPUTATION AND PROSPERITY, UNTIL 2116, WHEN ITS FOUNDER WAS CONVICTED ON MURDER CHARGES.

"*Murder?*" Korden asked. "Who did she murder?"

A PRIVATE INVESTIGATOR LOOKING INTO THE DEATH OF ONE OF HER SUBORDINATES' CHILDREN. HERE IS WHERE INFORMATION BECOMES VAGUE ONCE MORE, DESCENDING INTO RUMORS. THE YOUNG SON OF A DISGRUNTLED FORMER BRG EMPLOYEE DIED BY WHAT POLICE DEEMED A SUICIDE, BUT THE FATHER CLAIMED THE BOY'S DEATH WAS RETALIATION BY MISS MOAMBATI AFTER HE CONTACTED THE FBI ABOUT HER BUSINESS PRACTICES. WHEN THE OFFICIAL INVESTIGATION TURNED UP NOTHING, HE HIRED A DETECTIVE, BUT THIS MAN ALSO DIED BY WHAT INITIALLY LOOKED LIKE SELF-

INFLICTED METHODS. HOWEVER, A RECORDING OF THE DEATH FOUND ON THE BODY HELD TERESE MOAMBATI'S VOICE. EVEN THOUGH SHE HAD AN UNIMPEACHABLE ALIBI AND ALL PHYSICAL EVIDENCE WAS CIRCUMSPECT, THE RECORDING WAS ENOUGH TO CONVICT HER. IT REMAINS ONE OF THE STRANGEST CRIMINAL PROSECUTION CASES IN HISTORY.

"Wow," Korden whispered. "Guess I shouldn't be surprised though. Anyone responsible for creating those headbands would have to be a monster."

I AM NOT CERTAIN THAT'S THE CASE. YOU SEE, SHE WAS—

"Why is it you wish to study this historical human female?" Zeega interrupted. "Do you truly believe there is a link between her and this Moambati of the Skyreach?"

IF YOU'LL WAIT, THERE'S MORE TO—

"I don't know. But it would seem like a pretty big coincidence otherwise, don't you think?"

YES, BUT YOU MUST COMPREHEND WHAT—

"Zeega does not believe in coincidences. There is only what is, and what isn't."

I REALLY MUST INSIST THAT YOU LISTEN TO—

"That's what I'm saying, it *can't* be a coincidence! Stone, could you finish the story and tell us what happened to this woman?"

WHAT A NOVEL IDEA, the computer said stiffly. TERESE MOAMBATI WAS SENTENCED TO TEN YEARS IN PRISON, BUT DIED IN A RIOT SIX MONTHS LATER, LEAVING ALL HOLDINGS OF BRAINWARE RESEARCH GROUP TO HER TWIN DAUGHTERS.

Korden sat up so fast he banged his head on the wagon's undercarriage. "Twin daughters? You didn't say anything about that!"

THEY WERE IRREVELANT TO THE NARRATIVE UNTIL NOW. BORN IN 2097, DENISE AND CHARLOTTA ALCIMA HAD A TUMULTUOUS RELATIONSHIP WITH THEIR MOTHER, LIVING ALMOST ENTIRELY WITH THEIR FATHER. BY ALL ACCOUNTS, THEY WERE AS BRILLIANT AS TERESE, GRADUATING EARLY FROM HIGH SCHOOL AND TWO YEARS INTO DOCTORATE STUDIES WHEN THEY TOOK CONTROL OF BRG AT THE AGE OF 20 AND CHANGED THEIR LAST NAME TO CAPITALIZE ON THEIR MOTHER'S SUCCESS. AFTER THREE YEARS UNDER THEIR GUIDANCE, THE COMPANY WAS BACK ON TRACK AND MORE PROFITABLE THAN EVER. IT WAS UNDER THEM THAT THE FIRM WAS REBRANDED MOAMBATI INDUSTRIES, INC, AND MANY NEW PATENTS BEGAN TO ROLL OUT.

"Then search your resources for information on the mind-controlling device," Zeega ordered.

I AM CAPABLE OF DOING MY JOB, Stone snapped. WHILE A PATENT WAS FILED FOR A SIMILAR DEVICE CALLED A 'MUSCLE MEMORY'—MEANT TO FACILITATE THE USE OF TRANSPLANTED LIMBS BY THOUGHT—I WAS UNABLE TO LOCATE ANY RECORD OF ONE WITH THE SPECIFIC USAGE THAT TARMON DOAKS EMPLOYED ON MR. BRIGHT. WHICH MAKES SENSE, BECAUSE IT VIOLATES MANY PRECEPTS OF THE CEREBRAL RESEARCH STANDARDS ACT OF 2089. THIS MODEL MIGHT HAVE BEEN DEVELOPED IN SECRET, BUT FOR WHAT PURPOSE? AND, IF ONE EXISTS, LOGIC DICTATES THERE WERE OTHERS.

Korden swallowed against a hard knot in his throat. "Do you have a picture of them also? Her daughters?"

SEARCHING... AFFIRMATIVE. THIS WAS A PUBLICITY PHOTO USED FOR THE COMPANY REBRANDING ANNOUNCEMENT.

The two blackenfolk women that appeared in his head were visible from the neck up. They looked exactly alike except for their hairstyles and expressions: the one on the left with braids along her scalp, grinning sunnily; the one on the right sporting a prim bob and a dour smirk. Both were far younger and lovelier than their mother, but with the same unflinching ardor in their eyes.

They also seemed instantly familiar to him, and he suspected why.

"What happened to these two women? How did they die?"

Stone beeped as he sifted through information. SEARCHING...UNKNOWN. THEY LIVED DURING THE TURBULENT PERIOD HISTORY HAS LABELED 'THE PURGES,' WHEN SOCIETY BEGAN TO COLLAPSE. RECORDS FROM THIS TIME ARE CHAOTIC AND INCOMPLETE AS MASS MIGRATION OCCURRED. THIS PHOTOGRAPH IS ONE OF THE LAST KNOWN OF THE MOAMBATI SISTERS.

Zeega studied him with all five of her eyes. "Why does this information trouble you?"

Korden met her multifaceted gaze. "Because I think I've been dreaming about them."

4

Rand lifted the bandage to examine the crude stitches on either side of Lillam's shoulder in the lantern light. He was no doctor, but the edges of the small entry wound appeared much redder and more swollen than the exit on the back. "It *could* be getting better, I suppose. Might help if we could keep the sand out of it."

"You can't keep the sand out of anything here." Lillam pushed a sweaty clump of hair from her brow. She was sleeping in another of his tunics and not much else, revealing a long expanse of leg that was glorious even with the carpet of stubble growing on it. "I think it's under my *eyelids*."

"Yes, but..." Rand used the last of his water ration for the day to rinse grit out of the wound, then replaced the bandage with a fresh one from the kit Korden had brought back. He frowned as he wrapped the cloth around the appendage. "Are you sure you don't want to let Korden at least look at it...?"

She yanked up the shoulder of the tunic as she glared at him. The shadows inside their tiny lean-to caused the hollows under her eyes to look as deep as his brother's.

"Sweetlove," he began, choosing his words carefully, "this is going to be a long journey with plenty of unpleasantness, so I have to ask...what's the point of this grudge?"

"The point is that he's a disgusting Crafter, and I want nothing to do with him."

"But *why*? For most practical purposes, his powers appear more useless than harmful." He felt a small pinch in the back of his mind as he said this, a sharper version of that tingle he'd first experienced when she told him about the baby. It had happened again during the strange balancing act he'd performed on the edge of the speeding wagon when they rescued Korden from Doaks. And yet another time during their escape from the Incarnates, as Korden stopped a projectile just before it hit him in the back.

And it was *Korden that did that...right?*

Rand immediately shoved the voice that asked this to the back of his mind without even considering the implications of such a question.

"You've been angry with him as well," Lillam pointed out, drawing him back to the discussion.

"Yes, because I disagree with his philosophies, and I'm angry at his actions. But I don't dislike him for being what he is. Can you please explain this irrational hatred so many people harbor for Crafters?"

Lillam sat up, wincing as the motion jostled her arm but eager to accept the challenge. "They...they worship some pagan god!"

"So do the Saint of Christ folks, but you don't see them getting run out of every town under threat of stoning."

"Because they keep to themselves! The basic principle of the Aged Lord's Writ of Elderly Governance is that you shouldn't provoke war with the Filament! But that's all *his* kind does! And they've been doing it for hundreds of years!"

Rand let a narrow smile onto his face as he laid a hand on her stomach. "Uh, excuse me miss'um, I think the Writ also says a thing or two about conceiving children, but you seem to be skimming right over that part."

Lillam scowled. "Don't you pass judgment on me, Rand Holcomb."

"Isn't that what you're doing to him? A sinner can't very well use sin as an excuse to hate someone."

She blushed (and oh, how he wanted to smother those blooms of color in kisses) but ruminated for a long moment before answering. "I can't speak for anyone else, but I guess…what it comes down to for me is…what makes *them* so special? With all the people in this world suffering, who decided that these certain people get such abilities? It's not right. It's not *fair*."

He chuckled. "So what you're saying is that you're jealous of a sixteen-year-old boy."

"You're twisting my words around!"

"And you're hiding behind semantics."

"Never your mind." She flopped back down on her side away from him, pulling the mass of blankets over her.

He switched off the lamplight and slid in behind her, conforming his body to hers. Beneath them, the sand held a hint of the day's warmth, but it would seep away quickly now that the sun was down. The desert night was quiet except for the constant scratch of the wind outside their tent and some muttered conversation over by the wagon, where Korden bedded down. He must be talking to that mind-rock, or maybe the weird, spongy creature that followed him around like a lost puppy now.

Rand slid an arm around Lillam's waist to caress her stomach, imagining the strange miracle that was taking place inside it. What did his child look like, deep inside her? Could it sense his touch?

"Do you feel any different?" he asked.

"Just tired and sick all the time."

And that could be from the shooter wound, he thought. The truth was, neither of them knew what to expect from this state called 'pregnancy.'

She said nothing else for so long, he thought she'd drifted off. Then she said quickly, "I'm not a hypocrite. I know having this child is unforgivable. That we'll be sentenced to the Three Fires. But it doesn't *feel* like a sin. It...it makes me happy. What about you?"

"Yes, of course," he said, wincing at the forced cheerfulness in his voice. But he couldn't help feeling reticent. This child was nothing they'd planned, nothing he'd wanted. Thus far, all it had done was take from them. He simply couldn't muster her newfound enthusiasm.

But maybe if he faked it for long enough, it would eventually be true.

Her body stiffened. He waited for her to press him. But when she spoke, it was to say, "We'll have to come up with a name sooner or later."

Rand's brow furrowed in the darkness. He hadn't even considered the idea. What a monumental undertaking, to bestow a moniker upon a living, breathing human being. What if it didn't suit her? What if she didn't like it?

In front of him, Lillam asked tentatively, "What will we do if we get there...to the Skyreach...and it isn't safe after all?"

"Then we'll keep running. Whatever we have to do."

She squirmed around to face him. Her lovely eyes were the only part of her face visible in the dark tent. "Speak true, Rand: did we do the right thing? Leaving Ida, our homes...?"

He didn't answer until he'd found the one thing he truly believed about the mess his life had become. "The way I see it, back in Ida, I wouldn't've ever been able to lay with you like this. We would've lived our lives separated by a wall, stealing each moment together. So right now, at this very second…I'm exactly where I want to be. The rest, we'll figure out when we have to."

It must've been the right thing to say, because she moved closer and her lips found his in the dark.

5

If there was one bit of credit Heater could bestow upon the *Exatraedes*, it was their efficiency at breaking down camp each day at sunset, so they could get on the move.

Then again, there were damn near 250 of them now, so all those extra hands should be good for *something*. Standing atop a sand dune at the head of the demon contingent, Heater couldn't even see the end of the makeshift tents and awnings and vehicles whose windows had been hastily covered with scrap metal to keep the sun out.

Yes sir; it was a formidable force that Regent Torgas had put at his disposal.

Too bad they would be just as useless as the tits on a crone if Heater couldn't find a way to spur them on faster.

At first, he'd ordered the *Exatraedes* to chase the kid around the clock, without stopping. Korden's merry band wasn't keeping a very fast pace in that heavy wagon, and the Incarnates could sense them stopping each night also. Heater believed that, even with these sand canyons forcing them to go out of their way to continue the pursuit—and he could swear the damn things were moving in front of them somehow—they would've been able to run down their quarry long before now if he'd gotten his way. But these poor widdle demons had more trouble with the sun than an albino eating a popsicle (a joke Heater didn't entirely understand no matter how many of the voices in his head assured him it was hysterical). Their skin blackened after long exposure, then liquefied into a substance like tar. And if it got in their bare eyes, they couldn't do anything but curl up into a useless ball. The various platoon leaders among them insisted on calling a halt at sunrise each morning, in order to hide in the shade.

So they bivouacked during the day and rode carefully at night, while the boy's group did the opposite.

There was a certain yin-and-yang aspect to that which Heater appreciated.

Loathe, on the other hand, did *not*. The entity paced the inside of their shared mind, eaten up with impatience to get a grasp on Bright's scrawny neck. The ground they gained, little by little, hour by hour, did nothing to soothe the multi-voiced presence in his head.

To keep his mental roommate from blowing a gasket, Heater strode through the camp, barking orders, urging the demons to hurry. Within minutes, most of the Incarnates had their shelters packed and were running toward their rides. They drove whatever ancient vehicles they'd scraped together before making their way into the Valley of Bones, all of them maintained and fueled by a constant stream of rendered fantasies from he and Loathe, courtesy of the hundred imaginative souls they'd devoured in Ida.

Some of the newer arrivals piloted contraptions they called 'sand skiffs,' which looked like Yukon dogsleds with a closed-in cockpit, pulled by teams of the tentacled riftling creatures. And there were more of them coming all the time, from the north and south, joining the growing convoy as it raced across the desert. Torgas told him in their last long-distance tête-à-tête that Heater might have as many as 700 Incarnates by the time they hit the Skyreach.

An army. One they could use to discover the truth behind this 'Moambati' that had divided the nation in two. Then, once they'd repaid their debt to Torgas and sucked all the juice from the boy's imagination, Heater planned to return home, create himself a brand-new shooter factory, wave goodbye to Loathe, and spend the rest of his life getting obscenely rich.

As he strutted toward his own conveyance—a rustbucket Dodge Ram with mismatched tires and a smoke-belching engine that made him miss his hovertrikes sorely—he spotted a group of five Incarnates lazing under an improvised canopy. Heater beelined toward them so fast his boots kicked up sprays of sand with each step.

"What's the deal, boys?" he demanded. "You hittin the snooze button, or do you maybe wanna pick your worthless asses up and get movin?"

None of them spared him a glance, but the closest—a demon wearing cracked ski goggles and with only a few clumps of red hair left in his rotting scalp—growled, "We're tired of taking orders from you, parasite."

Fighting against his every instinct, Heater took a breath to steady himself before speaking. He understood that these Incarnates didn't want him around. They'd been doing their thing for countless eons, burning up the cosmos one plane at a time, and then here comes an outsider telling them how to do it better. It would piss anyone off.

But this constant insubordination must be quelled. Heater just needed to make sure he didn't cause an all-out mutiny by flying off the handle. He and Loathe still needed their help.

For now, anyway.

"Then it's a good thing you ain't takin orders from us," he said calmly. "You're takin orders from Torgas, same as always." *Who just happens to be takin* his *orders from us.*

The red-headed demon leapt to his feet. One of Loathe's voices informed Heater that he looked a little like someone named Ron Howard with twenty pounds of extra muscle and stage 3 bowel cancer. He squared up to Heater in his piecemeal armor as the rest of his crew clustered around him like sniveling lackeys backing up the schoolyard bully. "You are a disgrace to the Filament," the Incarnate declared. "Degenerate scum that revels in the dreams of humanity instead of destroying them. When the Deadfather finds out that Regent Torgas has us answering to the likes of you, his torture will be unequaled."

"That's great." Heater suppressed a grin. These grunts were unaware that Moambati had severed all communication with the Filament high command for more than a decade and a half; Torgas had been careful to keep that secret to himself. For all they knew, he was looking at the last of their kind right here. "Until that happens, let's keep in mind that our interests are aligned. We all want the kid the dead, right? There's no reason to squabble."

"Squabble with this, parasite."

The Incarnate moved fast, yanking a rusted blade from his belt and driving it deep into Heater's guts.

Pain ripped through him, its very existence as shocking as its intensity. He hadn't felt *actual* pain—other than Loathe's never-ending hunger—since Bright shoved a fiery fist down his throat, made him wreck his ride, then left him burned and broken and bleeding in the forest. Though it'd never expressly been part of the agreement with Loathe, Heater kind of believed he was free of such physical mundanities when he accepted the entity into his mind.

His surprise must've shown, because the Incarnate turned to his flunkies and roared, "See, he's just a man! Kill him!"

look out stop him get away danger Loathe babbled inside his head, a Greek chorus of panic.

Heater stepped back with the dagger sticking out of his stomach and reached into his imagination. A split second later, a waist-high shape popped into existence next to his attacker, a beast with the body of a lion, but whose head was nothing but a square opening full of whirring blades. This woodchipper-on-four-legs pounced at the ginger Incarnate, bearing him to the ground. Black ichor sprayed across the sand as he began to scream.

Within seconds, the body on the ground was little more than a chewed-up torso. Heater's creation squatted beside him like a sphinx as he looked at the other four demons. "Any of you think I'm just a man?" Without a word, they hurriedly went about packing up their camp. Heater waited until they scrambled away before releasing the creature from reality.

He moved toward his ride. Strength was draining from his legs, but he was determined not to stumble while the eyes of every *Exatraedes* in the troop were upon him. When he was hidden inside his own tent, he wrenched the knife from his guts with a shaking hand.

The pain made his eyes water. Blood flowed over his fingers and down the front of his leather *jhaken* at an alarming rate. But, worst of all, the illusion he cloaked himself in—that of his long-dead twin brother—flickered momentarily, revealing the blackened, shattered form within.

"What is this?" he gasped. "Aren't we...beyond all this?"

still a man flesh and blood body doesn't change must protect us

It made sense, now that he truly considered it. He hadn't been able to heal his previous injuries, only mask them, because Loathe strictly dealt in the abstract. "Then what the fram are we supposed to do about *this*?" he demanded, pressing a fist to the gushing hole in his stomach.

fix it make something up repair the illusion pretend it away

Heater frowned. He couldn't wrap his mind around the suggestion until several of the personalities that made up Loathe's infinite psyche explained it in terms of computers and software.

A patch. That's all it was. Glitch repair. Heater Kay Version 2.1. He closed his eyes, used his imagination, and simply...overwrote the injury. The new flesh was nonsensical—green and scaly and not remotely human—but it stopped the pain, corked the bleeding. Some part of him understood this solution was no different than slapping some duct tape on a lemon to get it off the showroom floor, but he was okay with that. Once he got the kid, it wouldn't matter. *None* of it would matter, because with the power stored in that brat's head, he would be able to set everything right. Get his life back on track.

Is that even you *talking anymore? Or is it all just Loathe?*

He didn't know. He'd never understood exactly where he ended and the entity began. Loathe could obviously take control of their shared body whenever it wanted, could feed on him in a pinch, but it couldn't be completely self-sufficient. There had to be some sort of symbiosis—of... *collaboration*—otherwise it wouldn't need a host in the first place. The one thing Heater was sure of is that all their renderings came directly from his consciousness, and he'd long suspected Loathe would be powerless without someone to do the imagining for him.

Heater's hands shook, but now the weakness came from hunger. Covered in blood, Heater tore out of the tent, stomping to the horse trailer attached to the back of his truck. At the door, he took in the nine remaining townsfolk he'd brought from Ida as emergency rations. Most of them were near death from dehydration and heat exhaustion.

Loathe had drained a sizeable chunk of that dipshit burg, enough to leave Heater juiced out of his mind. It wasn't *quality*, as with that single taste of the kid, but it was definitely *quantity*. However, providing fictional fuel to this fleet of vehicles was emptying the coffers, and the imagination he'd just expended hadn't helped.

When they saw him, those prisoners that were capable pled for mercy. Loathe drained two of the ones that didn't move—the others bleated in terror as their fellow captives' heads imploded—and despaired at the tiny kick of imagination their minds provided. Heater fought to reign the entity in as it reached out for three more.

"We're gonna be outta chow long before we leave this desert unless you make it last," he warned.

your fault do not question us keep moving catch him

The desperation in that choir made him (or whatever part of him was still *only* him) a tad uncomfortable. "Are you sure?" he pressed. "When we catch the kid…and suck him dry…are you *sure* it'll be enough? To do everything you promised?"

absolutely you'll have it all every wish trust us

Heater hesitated for the barest of seconds before climbing into the truck and speeding into the hazy desert night with his growing army behind him.

A DIFFICULT
DECISION

1

"Definitely a caravan of *some* sort." Doaks adjusted a wheel on top of his farviewers as he peered through the scratched lenses. "I count...six wagons, maybe fifteen or sixteen trailhands. Not sure how they got way out here without any beasts to pull 'em, though."

"Maybe their wagons are some kind of autos," Korden suggested.

"Don't appear so, but I guess looks can always be deceiving. Sometimes it seems there ain't no end to the wonders of the old world."

They lay on their stomachs at the crest of a high sand dune with Meech and Rand, studying the group that waited ahead of them from beneath a blanket, so the sunlight couldn't sear their bare flesh. They'd just eaten lunch when Korden sensed the other *mohols* ahead, and Doaks powered down Gwenita so they could scout ahead for danger on foot.

"They could be loaded with cargo," he added wistfully. Sweat trickled down his rough cheeks. "Mighta been nice to trade with 'em, but *somebody* went and burned everything I owned of any value."

Rand snatched the farviewers and pressed them to his own face. "I don't like it. They're stopped in the middle of the day. They could be brigands, lying in wait for travelers."

"Not a very lucrative business model, eh? The chances of runnin across someone out here are slim."

"Exactly, which is why it makes me so uneasy that we have. Let's keep out of sight and go around them."

"Normally I'd be inclined to agree, however…" Doaks raised a hand to point. "See that break in the crevy just past them? That might be the only crossin to the south for a hundred spans, and the ion station we need is a bit farther on. We circle around yonder caravan, we're gonna be forced back to the north. Might as well look for someplace else to charge up if we do that. And I got no idea how far that is."

I CONCUR WITH THIS ASSESSMENT, Stone said.

"Thanks, li'l fella!" Doaks shot a toothy grin at Korden, his hungry eyes going right to the computer around his neck. "Really like that doodad. Any chance I could buy—?"

"*No*," Korden said firmly.

"All right, all right, don't get yah dungarees soggy."

"Then h-how long before we're…ya know…d-dead?" Meech rolled over onto his back as he spoke, wrapping both arms around his stomach and grimacing. A fierce attack of the gimmies had been on him since he woke up this morning, and his *mohol* was a jumbled mess. "Power-wise, I m-mean."

"I'll have to hook up the first battery tomorrow mornin,

if not sooner." Doaks shrugged as a gust of wind blew sand into their faces. "After that…it's anybody's guess."

Rand gave a conceding nod. "Then we go past them. No matter who they are, it's not like they could hurt us anyway. Korden'll just crush them into a little ball if they try anything, right?"

"I can't do that!" Korden exclaimed.

"Sure you can, I watched you do it to that Incarnate in Ida a few days ago. You killed all three of them without lifting a finger."

"Yeah, but those were Incarnates! I won't use my artcraft to hurt *people*!"

Doaks rubbed one of his sagging jowls. "My cheek would disagree. That was quite a wallop yah gave me back in the detention cell. 'Bout tore my head off."

Korden looked down as shame burned across his face. "That shouldn't have happened. My emotions got the better of me. I…I apologize."

"Then what about when you threatened Hildan? Or *me*?" Rand asked.

"Those were just…words."

"So it's all right to scare people to get what you want."

"That's not…I never would've attacked you!" Korden insisted.

"Unless your emotions get the better of you."

"W-would you leave the li'l drude alone?" Meech begged.

"No, I won't. Because we've been putting our necks on the line to save him ever since we laid eyes on him. I'd like to figure out when we can count on him to do the same for us." Rand pushed up on his elbows to glare at Korden over Doaks's back, letting a shaft of burning sunlight jab at them beneath the blanket. His aura blazed with frustration, the one emotion he seemed capable of anymore when speaking to Korden. "You're telling me, if one of those people down there turned out to be dangerous, you wouldn't protect us?"

"No! I...I would do what I had to, but I just..."

"You just *what*?"

Korden searched for the words to explain. About how it'd felt to burn Heater from the inside out. Or to beat up those scared, angry men back in Ida. The last thing he wanted was to give these people another reason to fear him by admitting that his artcraft was growing beyond his control, thanks to these strange dreams. "I don't want to hurt anybody," he reiterated.

"Prob'ly better if they don't see the kid or the woman anyway," Doaks interjected, before Rand could harangue him any further. "I can hang back a ways with them in the wagon, while the two of yah go ahead with a talkie and see what yah can find out."

"If they d-don't chop us into pieces, then it's s-safe for you?" Meech asked.

"Settle on, I'm only tryin to be logical. Better we find out if they have any tricks up their sleeves before we bring Gwenita too close."

"We'll do it," Rand agreed. "But you better promise me you'll get Lillam out of here if anything goes wrong."

"I'll look after her like she was my own, rubo."

"Yeah, that's what I'm afraid of."

2

Lillam was uncomfortable being left alone with the boy and the driver. She pushed herself into the rear corner of the wagon, wanting to fade into the wall, but that was impossible to do after the driver made the bonnet transparent somehow. This allowed the blindingly bright sun to stream inside, but at least the heat didn't come with it.

Empty desert yawned around her. This was by far the most desolate place she'd ever seen in her life. It made her feel small and insignificant, turned all her problems into meager whimsy by comparison. This harsh place had existed here long before she was born, and would be here long after the life inside her died.

However soon that might be.

With the walls invisible, she could also see the tentacled creature perched on the roof above her head, as though suspended in midair. She'd all but forgotten about that hideous little beast; it gave her the willies also. As though able to hear her thoughts, the creature shifted and lowered its glistening black head to stare in at her with all five of its unblinking yellow eyes.

Its young master stood a few paces away from her with their toadish driver, both peering across the sandy plains to where Rand and his brother approached the mysterious caravan.

In truth, those two looked a little chummy, considering one had supposedly held the other captive a mere week ago. That story always sounded fishy to Lillam; how could someone hold a Crafter as powerful as the boy against his will anyway?

It just went to prove what her mother always said: you couldn't trust anything that came from the mouth of an Upper-lover.

Hate him all you want, but he's been far more supportive of you and the baby than worshippers of the Aged Lord, a small voice in the back of her head pointed out. Images of Kasa Webb floated through her mind, the Matron's harsh words and needless cruelty. The townsfolk who'd taunted and thrown food at her while she was locked in the stocks. She suspected the angry, jeering faces of her friends and fellow Ida citizens would be burned into her memory for the rest of her life, would replay behind her eyelids every time she tried to sleep.

After a few minutes of staying away from the other inhabitants of the wagon, worry for the father of her unborn child superseded her discomfort. She moved forward to get a better view of Rand's progress, wincing at the pain in her shoulder. The wound throbbed with a sickly heat, although she'd told Rand it felt better to keep him from worrying over her.

The boy—Korden—glanced over his shoulder as she drew closer, giving her what was probably meant to be a comforting smile. "Don't worry, he'll be all right."

"It should be *you* out there," she spat, relishing the way his grin faded. "You were supposed to be the one protecting us. That was the deal. That's why he smuggled you in to hear that speaking box of Hildan's. And if anything happens to him…it'll be *your* fault."

She waited for him to speak, maybe even to use his misbegotten magic on her, to prove right all the stories she'd heard about his kind since she was a girl younger than him. But he only walked away, up the wagon and out onto the control deck.

The driver looked at her. "Hey lady, I don't know if yah picked up on this, but he's a sixteen-year-old kid."

"Says the man who enslaved him."

"Yeah, I *enslaved* him. Made him do *my* bidding. I didn't sit on my duff and expect him to solve all my problems. That's too much responsibility for anyone, let alone a pre-ager." His eyes cut down to her stomach. "Aged forbid somebody ever puts that kinda pressure on the spawn yah got growin inside there, eh?"

Lillam looked away from him and put a protective hand over her belly as the talkie crackled.

3

Rand shifted the improvised umbrella higher on his shoulder, seeking a better angle to block the sun. They'd created the sagging shade from burlap and thin sticks of cordwood and, though it might keep their flesh from cooking on their bones, carrying it was a chore. Already his tunic was sopped with sweat under the arms and around the neck.

He twisted his head around to make sure Meech was within the canopy's shade behind him. "Are you *certain* you're up to this? I told you, you could've stayed back in the wagon with the others."

His brother had stopped shivering (and how he could be cold in this heat, Rand would never understand), but he took plodding steps through the sand, as though each foot were weighted. "This is...the whole reason...I came, man," he panted. "To be the kid's bodyguard."

"The kid doesn't need a bodyguard. And you're not going to be much help if I have to carry you out of here."

Meech turned red-rimmed eyes on him to give a sickly grin. The bruise along his jaw from the beating he'd taken in Ida was no more than a shadow now. "Drude...when've you ever had to carry me?"

Rand rolled his eyes but refrained from telling his brother that he'd done nothing *but* carry him for two decades and counting.

The argument was moot at this point anyway. Ahead of them, across a short stretch of shimmering, heat-blurred sand, sat the six wagons of the caravan. Rand squinted at them in the glaring sunlight. They were giant, wooden transports, each with six spoked wheels as high as his chest. The kind of cart that requires a team of oxen to pull, but the yokes jutting off the front were empty. A covered bench provided some paltry shade for the driving team, but the rest of the conveyances consisted of nothing but deep, tarped beds full of whatever wares they were taking to market. The trailhands had been lounging in the cool shadows beneath the vehicles, but, when they caught sight of the hovering wagon, they scrambled out to shout and wave their arms over their heads like drowning swimmers. Now they hurried toward Rand and Meech, stumbling across the last fifty pargs of burning ground.

"Oh, thank the good Aged Almighty!" the first one to reach them panted. He was a wiry man with sloping eyes, wearing a sweat-stained white tunic, filthy brown leather overalls, and a wide, floppy-brimmed hat that kept a circle of shade around him at all times. "When we seen that floatin wagon, I thought fer sure we was hallucinatin!"

"No, it's real." Rand offered a hand. "I'm Rand Holcomb. This is my brother, Meech."

"Dabber Knox!" The man's enthusiasm never waned as he pumped Rand's hand, then gestured at the other trailhands gathering around them with their heads ducked down into deep collars. "This here's my crew! We're haulin textiles outta Payton Township, and...and *boy*, we're glad ta see you!"

"Payton Township. Is that anywhere near the Sky-reach?" Rand asked.

"Naw, not that far east. Just on the t'other side of the Valley."

"Well, do you know anything about the...the situation there?"

"Ya mean Moambati?" he asked, mangling the pronunciation with chopped syllables. "Just the rumors, but we'll tell ya what we heard! Anything ya need, *anything* at all, we're happy to oblige!"

Rand nodded toward the gigantic carts behind the trailhands. He had a terrible feeling about what was coming, based on the overwhelming gratitude of this man. "What's the problem, Mr. Knox?"

"Please, call me Dab." He lifted the front of his hat to wipe sweat from his brow, revealing a thatch of shaggy brown hair that was caked with sand. "It'd be quicker ta tell ya what's *not* the problem! We made the run from Payton to Skor a dozen times, and never had trouble like this. See, we got separated from the rest of our caravan, got lost in the crevies tryin to find 'em, and then a disease spread through all our ox, leavin us stranded. We been stuck out here a week!"

"Why didn't you start walking?"

"You funnin? *Walk* through the Valley of Bones? Even if we survived the heat, we didn't have the supplies ta make it out on foot. No sir, our best hope was ta pray someone'd find us. And, praise be, here ya are!"

"Praise be," Meech agreed. Rand shot him a dark look.

Dab grinned so big his cheeks seemed ready to tear down the sides. "Ya think that fancy wagon of yores has the power to tow a transport or two?"

"Oh, I…I don't know, it's not mine," Rand said.

The other man waved a hand in the air as though wiping the question away. "Ya know whut, it don't even matter, we'll have ta leave 'em here and hope we can find 'em later. But if ya could take us with ya, we'd be more grateful than ya could know!"

"Well…we're headed back in the direction you came from…"

"We don't care a bit where ya take us, we just gotta get outta this desert before we roast!" His wide grin slipped a few notches at Rand's hesitation. "If'n ya want payment, that ain't a problem. Get us ta civilization and I'll see yore took care of."

"It's not that." Rand spoke slowly to choose his words.

"Mr. Knox—Dab—we're being chased by…let's say, some *unsavory* types. Coming with us might not be the best course of action."

Dab stared at him in slack-jawed amazement. "We got enough water left fer 'bout four or five days, at most. I'd say yore about our *only* course of action. Whatever trouble yore in, we'd be glad to make it *our* trouble too, wouldn't we boys?" The rest of the trailhands nodded eagerly.

Rand sighed and clicked the button on the talkie. "I'll have to confer with the rest of my group."

4

"Would yah think on it for just one blasted second?" Doaks implored from the rear of the bonnet. His voice was screechy with urgency. "Even if yah discount that yah'd be sittin in each other's laps for the rest of the trip, do yah have any idea what sorta dent the weight of *fifteen* extra people would put on our power usage? We'd be lucky to go a half day without needin a recharge!"

"Don't hang the messenger," Rand said to his left. "I'm on *your* side. About this, I mean. I still think you're a pathetic scumbug."

"I'll take what I can get, rubo."

"I don't care." Korden crossed his arms in resignation. "We can't leave them here."

Doaks set his wide jaw as tones of aggravation bled into his aura. "Boy, remember how I told yah only two outta three caravans make it across this desert? Well, those poor schmuckies over there have the misfortune of bein the third. They're drownin, yah see? And if you try to rescue 'em, they'll pull us down, too."

"That doesn't mean we shouldn't try!"

"Fine, then tell me this: how are you gonna feed 'em? What are they gonna drink?"

THIS QUERY IS VALID. Stone sounded contrite. I CALCULATE THE ADDED STRAIN WILL DEPLETE OUR RESOURCES WITHIN 5.3 DAYS.

"Yah see?"

Korden paused a moment before giving the only argument he had left. "The Upper will provide."

"Oh, don't gimme that malarkey! If yah really believed that, yah never woulda needed my wagon in the first place! Yah woulda just *walked* across the damn desert!"

"Or maybe the Upper provided that, too."

Doaks gave a mean-spirited chuckle. "Yah religies are all the same. Don't matter if yah call 'im the Upper or the Aged, if somethin good happens, it's cause of the man in the sky. If yah luck turns sour, blame the Stranger."

"This is ridiculous." Rand's *mohol* was perfectly in tune with the other man's as their emotions reinforced one another in a sympathetic bond. He pointed at Korden. "You may be in charge of this expedition, but you're not the only one on it. You're taking chances with all our lives, so we should all get a say in it. Meech, what do you think?"

His brother sat on the cot at the front of the bonnet, hunched over and pale. "I'm with Korden, man. Always."

Rand sighed. "Of course you are. And I'm sure that thing on the roof agrees, too. But as for the rest of us—"

"I think he's right."

Rand, Korden and Doaks held a brief contest to see whose jaw could drop farther as they turned to Lillam where she sat in the corner, speaking into her lap.

"You're listening to *him*?" Rand demanded.

She looked up. Her eyes met Korden's before she jerked her gaze away. "I'm listening to myself. I just happen to agree with him."

"But Lillam, sweetlove, I don't think you understand—"

"Don't talk down to me. I understand the situation fine. Those men out there will die unless we help them."

"And I want to, but not if we're going to kill ourselves in the process!"

"Then think of some way around it! Isn't that what you do for your precious Mayor Hildan? Solve problems no one else can figure out?"

"Yes, I do. But sometimes solving the problem is about knowing when the problem can't be solved." Rand ran fingers through his overgrown hair. "Didn't we say we'd do whatever it takes to protect our daughter? Doesn't her safety have to come first?"

"Don't you dare use my child as an excuse to justify your actions!"

"*Your* child?" Rand flashed an exaggeratingly shocked expression. "She certainly wasn't *your* child when you convinced me to give up my life and everything I've worked for to come on this dimwit's quest!"

Lillam looked away so fast, the words might've slapped her. Her aura swirled with a complicated mixture of shame, anger and fear.

"Yeesh," Doaks murmured. "That one's gonna get you

kicked outta the tent for a few nights, my friend."

"But there *must* be something we can do," Korden insisted. He was so tired of leaving people to die in his wake.

Rand held out a hand to him. "Then you tell us, Mr. Artcraft! You're the one with the magic! What can *you* do for them?"

Korden squeezed his eyes shut, ground his teeth, and clasped his hands as he tried to coax an idea out of his brain. But he could think of nothing, no way to use his power to help these people aside from a complicated level of conjuration that, at his level of mastery, would cause more problems than it solved. All this artcraft, all this willpower, all this creativity and faith, and so far, he'd only used them as blunt instruments, not good for much more than bashing and burning and destroying.

Maybe that was what the Upper required of him.

Doaks used the opportunity to move closer. "Boy, I don't pretend to understand this quest yah on," he said, speaking somberly, "but I see it's important to yah. And hells, maybe it's more'n just bunk, cause a whole mess of Incarnates are tryin to put an end to it. But one thing I *do* understand: when a goal is important enough…sometimes difficult decisions hafta be made. Mature, grown-up decisions. About how far yah willin to go. And what yah'd be willin to sacrifice."

"People die every day so that someone else can live," Rand added. "Aged Lord only knows how many people those Incarnates killed back in Ida just because you were there. If you're willing to sacrifice their lives for some great-er good, how are these people any different?"

Korden sat up straight and turned from one man to the other with calm resolution. "We're at least giving them water. I'll take half-rations for the rest of the trip."

"Me too," Meech said.

"I will also," Lillam agreed.

I AGREE, THIS COURSE OF ACTION SHOULD RESULT IN AN EXTRA THREE DAYS OF HYDRATION FOR THE STRANDED INDIVIDUALS.

"Voices in our head that don't need food or water don't get a vote." Rand looked around at them before tossing up a hand in defeat. "Fine, we'll...fill some waterskins for them."

"And why don't you be the one to give it to them?" Korden invited. "I'm sure they'll be eternally grateful."

5

Doaks slowed the wagon as they drew up to the caravan but said he didn't dare stop. Rand thought that wise—why prolong this any more than necessary?—but also questioned what it said about himself that he and the pint-sized swindler were suddenly in agreement about so much.

Well, at least Rand possessed the courage to stand behind his decisions and face the men he was denying. He waited alone on the rear deck, letting the sun sear his bare skin as a kind of penance while they hovered past the large transports, heading toward the break in the crevy. Knox and his crewmen emerged and ran alongside them, their friendly grins making Rand a little queasy. He assured himself that these men were rational beings; they would see the logic behind *you-or-all-of-us*.

"So how 'bout it?" Knox asked, the wide brim of his hat flopping with each step. "Can we hitch a ride?"

"I'm sorry." Rand marveled at how cold his own voice made the apology sound. "We just don't have the water."

The trailhands exploded in angry rabble.

Knox's friendly smile crumpled into a grimace. "You're killin us!" he shouted.

"As soon as we get to the far side of the Valley, we'll tell someone you're here." Rand hefted the waterskins they'd filled and tossed them over the side. "Here, this is all we can spare."

Knox caught one of the bladders, looked at it in disgust, then let it drop. "This won't do anything but prolong the agony! We need *help*, damn it!"

"And that's as much as we can give."

"Then to hells with you!"

"*Get 'im!*" someone else shouted.

An object flew out of the crowd and smashed into the bonnet beside Rand, a heavy piece of metal that rolled off the end of the deck. Then they were all pelting him with debris. *So much for rationality.*

"Stop, don't do this!" he pleaded, but the barrage intensified. Rand ducked and dodged while Knox and a couple of the other trailhands leapt at the wagon. They dangled from the sideboards, trying to clamber up.

"*Doaks, go!*" Rand shouted.

The wagon accelerated, the lurching motion so sudden that Rand flailed his arms to stay upright. The rest of Knox's men fell behind, and one of the trailhands hanging on the sideboards lost his grip and plunged into the sand. Rand pried at the other's fingers until he fell also. But Knox managed to swing a leg over and rolled onto the deck, his hat blowing away.

The caravan master scrambled to his feet while making a low growl in his throat. Rand charged at him, grabbed his shoulders, and tried to drive him off the back of the wagon as the sun ate at them. But Knox held the advantage in both size and muscle. He pivoted at the waist, braced the toe of one boot behind Rand's heel, and gave him a hard shove in the chest that sent him sprawling to the deck on his back.

"You miserable sacka curse!" Knox produced a short knife from his belt. He squatted over Rand, grabbed him by the tunic, and pressed the blade to his throat. "Let's see how much help you need when we take this wagon and leave you all to—"

The arm holding the knife was yanked away from Rand. Korden stepped up beside Knox, holding him by the wrist, then thrust a hip into his side. He performed a quick, oddly graceful maneuver that spun the other man head over heels and sent him flying off the back of the wagon. Rand twisted around in time to see him hit the sand with a surprised grunt, then looked at Korden.

"Like I said, I'll do what I have to." the boy told him. A dejected frown tugged at the his mouth as he walked back into the bonnet.

HORMONES

1

The landscape began to change at last, the hardpan rising sharply into long, flat-topped mesas that formed steep cliffs around them and littered the desert floor with boulders of all sizes. These bluffs gave them some much-needed relief from the sun, but interspersed among them were tall, monolithic formations of compacted sand, their bases as wide as the wagon and tapering to a slender column two-hundred pargs overhead, like the fingers of a spindly giant. As with the crevies, they were perfectly symmetrical and as smooth as sculptures.

"Those little pretties are what put the 'bones' in Valley of Bones," Doaks told them from the control deck one morning, as they skirted around a set of spires that jutted from the side of a mesa like pikes at the head of an army.

"What?" Rand asked. "I thought it was called the Valley of Bones because the sand would...well...scour the flesh from your corpse and just leave the bones."

Doaks spun on the pilot bench to shoot him a grimace. "That's a tad morbid, ain't it, rubo? Naw, people been seein those things out here for as long as anybody can remember. Some say they're the bones of huge lizard monsters that once roamed the world, but that's prob'ly bunk."

"Oh yeah, but sand spookies, *that's* gospel truth," Meech muttered. Their driver had brought up the legend at least three times a day since the start of their journey.

Doaks shot Meech the little finger, then said, "In any case, most folks avoid 'em. Bad omens and such."

Stone again pointed out that he could find no record of such features occurring naturally in this region, but admitted he could see no way—or reason—for a human to fashion them either. Korden studied the strange spires as they travelled the canyon trails between mesas, remaining wary until they emerged back into the open each time.

Gwenita sputtered to a stop amid a tight grouping of these escarpments the day after their encounter with the stranded caravan, as Doaks predicted. He estimated he would need ten or fifteen minutes to hook up one of the batteries. The rest of the company dispersed into the surrounding ravine, eager to be out of the wagon and thankful for the shade.

Korden left Meech and Rand bickering about lunch rations and walked back along the canyon, then ducked down another branch to empty his bladder. The dry desert wind moaned through the passage. Those tapering pillars jutted in all direction from the foundation of the cliffs, giving the impression that he was walking through a forest in which all the leaves and branches were stripped from the trees. It might've been beautiful, but he couldn't shake the nervousness they inspired.

Then, as he finished up and relaced his dungarees, the hairs on the back of his neck rose.

Eyes. He could feel eyes on him, the sensation very much like the monteela attack back in the redwood forest. Korden turned his head, looking up and down the canyon, but neither saw nor sensed anything to cause alarm. Stone confirmed his findings, using the very limits of Korden's eyes and ears to scan for danger. Was he imagining things? Feeling rattled, he moved back in the direction of the wagon, craning his neck back to study the top of the bluffs high above, and thought he caught a glimpse of color to his left—

Coming around the rolling foundation of one of the monoliths, he nearly ran into Lillam from behind.

She stood on the trail, dressed in another set of Rand's too-large clothing and the slippers Korden had found. Her aura was muddied with sorrow. Tears streamed from her eyes as she stared down at a grouping of three cacti sprouting from a crack in the mesa wall. Korden's chest tightened even more as he observed her weeping, the watched sensation momentarily forgotten.

"Are you all right? Is it your shoulder? Is it the baby?"

"No, I'm fine." She sniffled, wiped her face, and waved a hand at the cacti, which consisted of two large arms and a smaller clump between them. "It's just…they look like a little family…" Then she was off again, holding the back of one hand to her mouth to stifle the sobs.

Korden stood back, unsure what to do, while she got herself under control once more.

"Sorry. I'm…I'm sorry. I haven't quite felt like myself since…" Lillam laid a hand on her stomach, then leaned against the base of the wall and slid onto the ground beside the cactus family, the wide hem of Rand's tunic billowing around her legs. She murmured, more to herself than to him, "My mother always said a baby ties a woman's emotions into knots."

"It's called 'hormones,'" Korden told her. He didn't need Stone for this information; he'd once skimmed through a very clinical book about the mechanics of pregnancy in Skewtz's library. "They're chemicals in your blood that can change your mood."

She scowled up at him, her green eyes peering through a screen of messy blond locks. "What would you know about it?"

"Not much," he admitted. Instead of scurrying away as he usually did when she snapped at him, Korden walked to the opposite side of the trail and sat down across from her. "Although Stone could tell us anything you wanted to ask."

He knew he'd said the wrong thing when her frown deepened. She was the only one in the group that had 'withdrawn consent' and refused to let the computer communicate with her. "I don't want to hear from your mind-invading rock any more than I do you."

They sat in silence, and the surreality of the moment crashed down upon him. After spending his life in the village with a group of ancient old men, here he was, talking to an honest-to-Upper *woman*. And a gorgeous one at that. Even in the unflattering clothes, with sand plastered to her forehead and cheeks by sweat and her blond curls falling in greasy tangles, her beauty was impossible to hide. Korden had dreamed about a moment like this for years.

Although, in those fantasies, the females didn't hate him. Quite the opposite, actually.

It was for this reason that he pushed through her vehemence and asked tentatively, "What does it feel like?"

Lillam took a long time to answer, but he could see the anger fading from her *mohol* as she considered her answer. "It doesn't feel like anything," she told him. "No, that's not true. I feel...*something*. Some connection. But it might be all in my head. It's hard to explain."

"But it—she—will get bigger, right? And move around inside you?"

She nodded. "So I hear. But the first time she kicks me in the guts, I'll probably scream."

He snickered and was pleased when a tiny grin graced her chapped lips. "Are you scared?"

"Yes." The answer came so fast, it was more like he'd startled it out of her.

"About the birth? Or the Incarnates?"

"A little of both." She blinked a few times, and her gaze drew far away as she said softly, "But mostly...I'm scared that Rand will leave us, the same way his parents did to him."

"No!" The idea horrified Korden...but his thoughts went immediately to the couple's fight the day before about the lost caravan, and the way Rand had implied that he blamed her for them leaving Ida. "He would never do that!"

"Oh really? Do you know him so well?"

He didn't. In truth, he didn't know any of the people he was traveling with, had met them all barely two weeks ago. So he said the one thing he *did* know. "I see how much he loves you! And he'll love the baby, too!"

Lillam sighed. "You're so young."

He couldn't tell if this was meant as an insult. "What does that have to do with it?"

"Have you ever been in love?"

"No," he answered grudgingly.

"Then you don't understand that it isn't a guarantee. Love isn't made of steel. It's a fire that rages hot and steady at the outset, but always dies down in the end." Lillam lifted her face up to the river of orange sky visible over their heads between the mesa tops, but her *mohol* revealed the stark yellow fear running through her. "This baby isn't something we planned for. But as soon as I found out I was pregnant, I wanted it. I don't know why, but it…changed something inside me. Rand pretends to feel the same, but that change hasn't happened for him. Maybe it never will. He only left Ida because he loves me, just like you said. So what will happen when our love finally burns down to ash?"

She was right; these were matters far beyond Korden's experience. Any advice he tried to give would be platitude, gleaned from the many books he'd read. He decided to leave her with her thoughts. Korden rose and headed back toward the wagon, but, after taking a few steps, he turned back to tell her, "I think what you're doing is very brave."

Surprise burst onto her face, but he hurried away before she could respond.

2

Back at Gwenita, Doaks was worming out from the vehicle's undercarriage while Rand kept an eye on him and Meech reclined nearby. Korden had reached the main passage and was heading toward them when he saw the latter's gaze sweep over his shoulder.

Meech's eyes went wide. Terror flushed into his aura. "*Look on!*" he screamed.

Korden spun. One of the sand spires behind him had broken a quarter of the way up and was toppling over on top of him with ponderous inevitability. He broke into a shambling run, unable to take his eyes off the monolith as it picked up speed. The descent was eerily silent for something so large. Its lengthening shadow fell across him, outpaced him, and, as he gathered himself to try catching the mountain of compressed sand with artcraft, there was a screeching rumble from above. He looked up to find the column had become wedged in a narrow section of the canyon walls, the point jutting over him to create a natural ceiling. Scraped sand and rocks dislodged from the cliffside pattered down around him.

At the same time, a horrible grinding noise filled the ravine.

"Time to go, rubos!" Doaks called, pointing into the canyon ahead of them while he scrambled onto Gwenita's control deck.

The other monoliths shuddered in unison, jiggling and swaying like saplings in a stiff wind. Visible cracks raced across their bases as they began to tilt.

Rand cupped both hands around his mouth and bellowed for Lillam. She must've already been on her way though, because she careened into the main canyon before her name finished echoing. She faltered briefly as she took in the magnitude of the situation, then sprinted toward the wagon. Korden waited for her, the ground vibrating beneath his feet, and the two of them ran the last few pargs together, leaping onto the deck with Rand's help.

Doaks revved the engines and accelerated so fast it caused them all to stumble. They maneuvered through the ravine as the spires tumbled over around them. One of them crashed to the ground alongside the wagon, shattering into sandy chunks, the impact so tremendous they could feel it even through the hovering floor of the vehicle.

Korden leaned around the side of the bonnet to survey the danger ahead and caught sight of Zeega doing the same thing on her perch atop the vehicle. The giant columns seemed to be aiming for them as they collapsed, and Doaks was doing his best to maneuver around them. He swerved away from another that was swinging downward from their right with the finality of an axe, but Stone warned that they wouldn't escape its path. Korden swatted out with a blunt wave of artcraft as he had at the boulders back in Ida.

The mental weight of the monolith was staggering. They might be made of sand, but they were dense and thick. He gritted his teeth in pain but managed to deflect the column aside far enough that the tip only scraped the wagon's sideboard.

"I can see the end!" Rand shouted over his shoulder.

A hundred pargs ahead, the mesas dropped away and open desert yawned in front of them. But one of the spires was coming down across the mouth of the canyon, falling at a sedate, leisurely pace. Doaks poured on the speed until Korden had to slit his eyes against the rushing wind. They squirted beneath the monolith, its shadow casting them briefly into twilight, and cleared the other side with mere cupits to spare.

Doaks stopped the wagon once they were back among the dunes, then stumbled through the bonnet to the rear deck. "Well...I think we mighta worn out our welcome, eh?"

"W-what does *that* mean?" Meech asked, clutching his chest as he sank into the floor.

"That it was no accident," Rand interpreted. "Do you think it coincidence that all those columns collapsed together at the same time?"

"Maybe we did something," Lillam suggested as she stepped into the shade from the bonnet. "Created an echo or a vibration with the wagon's engine..."

"Sweetlove, they fell *toward* us."

I CALCULATE A 92.4 PERCENT CHANCE THAT TRAJECTORIES WHICH APPEARED TARGETED IN SUCH HIGH NUMBERS WERE BY DESIGN.

"But," Meech sputtered, "what could have the power to do that?"

"Sand spookies," Doaks stated, eliciting a groan from the rest of the group.

Korden looked back at the mouth of the canyon, now choked with debris, and thought about the eyes he'd felt watching him.

3

The ion station sat in the ruins of a small town mostly swallowed by the sands, the pump so buried they had to dig it out before they could use it. Then it took four agonizing hours to get Gwenita and the depleted battery charged, leaving them a half hour before sunset to get back on course.

An entire afternoon lost. Korden was acutely aware of each passing minute, lost ground that could never be recovered. When he opened the conduit's eye to the west and concentrated hard, he thought he could sense the collective auras of the Incarnates lurking at the very edge of perception, an undulating black carpet across the horizon much like the pathome that had smothered the blue waters of Lake Tay-ho. He even imagined he could feel Heater out there at the head of the demon army, sweeping toward him with that terrible smirk on his lips.

They'd been in the Valley of Bones seven days by this point, and their supply of firewood was gone. Korden conjured more ("Is that *real* wood?" Rand inquired, to which Korden assured him, "Close enough to burn."), and they huddled around the flames for a dinner of venison steaks and pickled halibard leaves. While they ate, Korden let them hear that afternoon's broadcast from the Prophet, bidding Stone to play it through Gwenita's speaker system:

"Greetings to all you listeners out there, the Weatherman is here to update you on that absolutely cr-*aaaaaa*-zy race that's going on in the Great Basin Desert! This is the most exciting thing to happen since ol' Helens blew her top again last century, and I just can't look away!

"If you're the betting type, then the smart money is definitely on the chas*ers* rather than the chas*ees*. The Incarnate army must be close to 400 strong now, and they keep narrowing the gap on whoever these unfortunate pilgrims are. I'd say they're about six days from running this group down, and that's only if our plucky heroes get their act together! This tiny band is bouncing around the desert like they're playing pinball, first shooting steadily east, dipping south for a couple hundred miles, and now they're hanging a 180 to head due north! Maybe they're lost, maybe they're nuts, but one thing's for sure, they're *great* entertainment! Stay tuned for the next update in 12 short hours!"

Meech broke the silence that followed. "*That* was the Prophet? I thought he'd sound...scarier."

"I'm glad someone's enjoying this situation," Rand sulked. "It's like he's watching a play."

"Do you think he can see us right now?" Lillam craned her neck back and forth to stare into the night around them. "Or hear what we're saying?"

"If he could, then he'd know who we are. He seems good at predicting big events from a distance, but can't give any sort of fine details."

Doaks caught Korden's gaze across the fire. "Headin north is gonna lose us more ground in this race, Cap'n. We should turn full east and try to get outta the Valley before they catch us. If this Moambati scares Incarnates as much as we keep hearin, then hopefully they'll give up."

Korden shook his head. "I need to speak to the Prophet first." When the other man opened his mouth to argue, Korden cut him off. "We'll have to pick up our speed and travel longer each day. You may have talked me out of helping those men, but you won't talk me out of this."

"We should vote," Rand insisted.

"Not about this. I gave you all a chance to go your own way before we left, and you chose to come with me. The Prophet is where I'm going. Anyone that doesn't like it is welcome to leave."

But, as he was about to discover, his traveling companions weren't the only ones that wanted to alter his course.

4

It was Tash this time, beckoning Korden into his home with gnarled hands, but the old man didn't get so much as a word out before Korden barked, "You're not Tash. You're not the Upper either. Who are you, and why do you keep invading my dreams?"

"'Invading?' What a harsh word ta use!" Tash looked stung as his blind eyes roamed. "Wasn't it my warnin that saved yeh from Loathe's ruse?"

"Stop hiding behind the faces of my family and *tell me the truth!*"

There was a pronounced pause, as if the world had come to a grinding halt. Then his old mentor and the walls of the *hucté* faded, becoming as translucent as the wagon's bonnet. Within seconds, he was no longer indoors, but standing in a vast meadow filled with low grass and pink-tinged buttercups. He could feel the sun on him and hear the babble of a shallow river that snaked through the field a few hundred pargs away. Beyond the stream, far in the distance, the plains led up to an enormous, rolling mountain range that stretched on and on across the horizon, dwarfing the Sierras in Tay-ho. The most prominent of the peaks in front of him was an oddly slanting vertex that seemed instantly familiar. Korden realized with a start that he was *inside* the painting from his previous dreams as he spotted two forms walking toward him across the meadow.

They were both females, a near mirror image of one another, like their foto.

They were also gorgeous enough to make his breath catch.

Their skin was a rich, deep, midnight black, utterly flawless, with faces that featured high cheekbones, wide noses and huge, almond-shaped eyes. But it was the ample curves of their bodies that his gaze was drawn to, sliding down their graceful necks, to full breasts, narrow waists, swelling hips, and along shapely legs bared below the thigh by the matching white frocks they wore, garments whose material was so sheer as to be almost see-through. They carried themselves with a lithe grace that made him think of dangerous predators in some far-flung jungle. The figure on the left wore the tightly-woven braids he remembered from the picture Stone had shown him, the one on the right sporting that shoulder-length bob of kinky black hair.

Looking at these exotic women as they approached barefoot through the flowers, Korden experienced that same excitement deep in his stomach, a yearning akin to hunger that would not, he suspected, be sated by food. That part of him which dangled below his belt grew hot and full, and he rushed to cover the growing bulge by clasping his hands over his groin.

"I know you," he said. "You're...Denise and Charlotta, aren't you? The daughters of Terese Moambati."

They grinned at him, standing a few pargs away with

their arms around each other's small waists, a gesture that made them appear young and innocent and even more attractive somehow. He held little experience judging the age of blackenfolk (or females in general) but he guessed these women to be a few years older than Lillam.

The one with the braids—Denise, he somehow knew with utmost certainty—smiled broadly and said, "Oh Korden, darling, you are truly as insightful as we expected."

"We left the trail, but the dots had to be connected," Charlotta rhymed. Their words were sprinkled with some lovely accent he'd never heard before, full of clipped syllables and stressed vowels. "Next, the remains of a town called Crested Butte are what you should seek."

"Keep going east from there, and you will find us waiting atop that peak." Denise held out an arm toward that crooked summit behind them, where something glittered in the sunlight like a beacon.

"But...how can you be real?" He swiveled his head back and forth between the pair, trying to meet their liquid umber eyes in equal measure. "You lived hundreds of years ago..."

"'Lived' is correct, that much is so," Charlotta began.

"But 'dead' is a state we didn't ever know," Denise finished with a wink.

"Please, stop that!" he pleaded. "No more riddles or rhymes!"

"Speaking this way stabilizes the bridge into your head."

"And such creativity helps us keep your artcraft fed."

"Then you *are* Crafters! I knew it!" Jubilation filled him. "You've been alive all this time, like the Olders! The Moambati at the Skyreach...that's you two, isn't it?"

They reached out with their free hands, each gently taking one of his, so the three of them formed a circle in the meadow. Their caress against his palms sent an exhilarating jolt up his spine.

Denise said, "All will be revealed once you truly reach our embrace."

"But if you don't stop these diversions, we may never meet face-to-face," Charlotta concluded, with a touch of what seemed like annoyance. Neither of them exhibited *mohols* in this dream world, so it was impossible for him to be sure.

"Why? Why have you been rushing me along? Why did you want me to leave my friends?"

Their expressions changed at this, smiles fading into a worrisome grimace for Denise and a thin-lipped glower for her sister.

"We need you with us, before the Incarnates catch you," Denise insisted patiently.

"Your companions, though, are not welcome, and the Prophet is a waste, too." Charlotta's words were cold.

"I am not yours to command," he told them, gently but firmly. "I will gladly meet you and hear your explanations after I cross the desert, but *I* decide where I go and with who."

Now Charlotta looked outright furious, dark brows lowered and full lips drawing back to bare teeth. Their hands grew warm in his as the conduit pulsed uncomfortably in his head.

"Make no mistake, Korden; these are demands." Denise sounded embarrassed as she broke eye contact with him to glance at her sister.

The pressure in his mind intensified sharply as energy poured into him, a flood of artcraft that he was helpless to refuse. He cried out in surprise but was able to hear Charlotta's last words as the dream crumbled around him.

"And if you won't see reason, we'll take matters into our own hands…"

5

Korden opened his eyes, surprised to be sitting up on his bedroll, but that was soon overshadowed by the nightmare unfolding in front of him.

By the light of the moon, he could see Meech pinned against the back door of Gwenita's bonnet above him, hoisted so high his feet dangled a full two pargs off the deck. His arms and legs were spread away from his body and moving even further as the limbs were cruelly pulled in opposite directions like a torture rack.

Korden's head pounded as a raging torrent of artcraft gushed through the conduit. That energy crackled on his skin, channeling through him like a lightning rod, acting with a mind of its own, as it had back in Ida.

"*Li'l drude,*" Meech gasped, his face contorted with pain from his impending dismemberment. Already his bony shoulders looked oddly distended. "*Korden, man, snap out of it! It's me!*"

SIR, WHAT ARE YOU DOING? YOU MUST STOP AT ONCE!

But he couldn't. Trying to close the conduit now would be like trying to stopper a waterfall with a cork. Every minute detail of the world jumped out in such sharp contrast that he could probably count each individual grain of sand in the dunes around them.

A whimper came from Meech's cracked lips. His eyes rolled back in his head.

Above the dying man's head, Korden saw Zeega's dark form scurry to the edge of the vehicle's roof. Her buzzing call barged into his mind and switched off that power as simply as blowing out a candle. Meech dropped to the ground and crouched on all fours, groaning.

"I'm sorry, I'm so sorry!" Korden ran to help him sit up.

"Don't worry, man, I'm all right," he insisted, although his *mohol* told a different story. "If anything, I think that mighta cleared my head."

"What happened? Can you tell me?"

He squinted. "I woke up and thought I heard you callin my name. Only it kinda sounded like...like it was in my *head*. I came to check on you and when I got close, you sat up, but your eyes were rolled back in your head. Next thing I know, I'm lifted off the ground and my wings are bein plucked off like a Wishing Day turkey."

Korden burned with shame. "I don't understand what happened, I was dreaming and..."

Meech gave a weak smile. "If that was a dream, I'd hate to see what your nightmares are like, drude."

"Why didn't you yell for the others?"

"I didn't want them to find out. Last thing Lillam needs is another reason to be scared of you."

"Thanks," Korden said.

After making sure his friend wasn't injured, he trudged away from their camp, shivering in the chilly desert night.

The wind was dead for a change, the haze in the air settled, and the moon cast a silvery shine on the sand. Doaks had warned them about straying too far into the tractless wastes, but right now, Korden didn't care.

Someone was always trying to manipulate him. Trick him. *Use* him. First Tash and Redfen and the Olders hiding the truth about his birth, then Loathe cajoling him with promises of his every fantasy. Heater kidnapping him. Doaks using him as a prop in his stage show. Now these dream women who claimed to be the leaders of a long-defunct technology company were taking control of his magic somehow. He thought about the early dreams, how euphoric they'd made him, and wondered if it'd all been a way to brainwash him, make him more susceptible to their suggestions and addicted to the artcraft they provided, the same way Meech was addicted to his jinko. He reminded himself that these women might very well be responsible for the headband that had enslaved him.

But none of these unpleasant thoughts could stop the warm ache from rising in his stomach when he recalled their stunning, ebony faces and shapely figures…the desires that had flitted through his mind, unbidden, when they'd taken his hands…

Unfortunately, Stone chose then to ramp up his sanctimonious chattering.

I DID TRY TO TELL YOU SUCH DREAMS MIGHT BE DANGEROUS. IT WOULD BE PRUDENT TO—

"*Stop telling me what to do!*" Korden grabbed the pendant that housed the computer, ripped it from his neck, then reared back and threw it as hard as he could. The tiny speck was lost immediately against the night sky, but Stone's fading voice reached his mind for another moment or two before passing beyond the range of his telepathy. Korden sank to his knees as a frustrated sob escaped him.

"You saw the human females again." He didn't have to turn around to know who the high, gargled voice belonged to. "These...*Moambatis*."

Korden wiped his eyes and composed himself as Zeega squatted beside him, her tentacles making an ornate design in the sand around her stubby body. All bunched up, she looked a little like the black cat that Del and Port kept when he was a child.

"I think they've been using my dreams to talk to me," he told her. "To keep me glutted with artcraft. So I would be dependent on them."

"What is it they want?"

"For me to come to them." He was already losing details of the dream, but the name of the place they'd told him to go—Crested Butte—burned in the center of his mind. He wondered if he would be able to find it on his map. "Alone."

"And will you do this, once you have crossed the desert?"

"I might not have a choice if I ever want to pass beyond the Skyreach." Korden took a shuddering breath while their perfect forms flashed through his thoughts. He knew from his reading that this preoccupation undoubtedly had as much to do with hormones as Lillam's mood swings and was, therefore, experienced completely against his will, but that didn't make him feel any less guilty for having the obsession. "Zeega, I need your help."

"You wish to use Zeega's call to dampen your abilities while you sleep, hoping that this will block their intrusions," the riftling surmised.

Hearing it said out loud caused panic to seize Korden. Which was further proof that he needed to end this reliance on borrowed magic. "Yes. And any other time I lose control. I...I can't trust myself anymore. Will you do it?"

She twisted her bulbous head to look up at him, her yellow eyes studying him—*reading* him—with piercing intent. "Korden is truly Zeega's...friend?"

The question surprised him, but he answered quickly. "I want to be."

"Then Zeega will do as you ask."

The hum filled his head. It seemed so irritating once upon a time, an attack on his mind, but now its presence was as comforting as a lullaby. The conduit narrowed until only a trickle of artcraft could pass through. If he could find a way to expend the vast reserves they'd pumped into his wellspring, he might start feeling like himself again.

"Thank you," he sighed. A new thought occurred to him, one he hesitated to voice until he remembered the riftling might be hearing it in his mind anyway. "The Incarnates... your masters...they're catching up to us."

"Zeega is aware."

"Do you still think they'll kill you?"

"Without question. After a lengthy torture session in front of the other broods. To discourage such transgressions."

"Then, if they catch us, you should run away. Save yourself."

Her wide mouth rippled and twisted, as though warring with itself. But before it could settle on an expression, three of her eyes cut away from him, toward the black desert beyond.

"Zeega and Korden are not alone," she hissed. "Something is out there."

Korden turned, scanning the night visually before using the conduit's eye. At first, he sensed nothing at all, just as in the canyon...but then a swirling aura darted across the dunes in front of them. No, not across them; *beneath* them, a band of emotional color that ran below the surface of the ground, cutting through the sand without the slightest resistance. He tried to focus on it, to glean what sort of creature the *mohol* might belong to, but it was quick and constantly shifting, flowing more like water than a physical form. After a second or two, he lost track of it.

"Let's find Stone and get back to camp," he said.

MAELSTROM

1

The morning after they reached the charging station, Korden and Doaks rousted the group before the sun even rose, both desperate to get on the move. Rand hurriedly packed up the improvised tent he shared with Lillam while she dressed in another of his tunics. He didn't even see the point in changing anymore; every article of clothing he owned now reeked of body odor and dried sweat.

Rand noticed her movements were slow and labored as she dressed. "You all right?"

"Just tired." She rubbed a hand across her belly but wouldn't meet his gaze. "And hungry all the time. You must've put a greedy little girl inside me."

He tried not to wince at the way she'd phrased that last statement. *You* must've put… Another reminder that he was as much at fault for their situation as she was. "We'll be out of this miserable land soon, I promise. Until then, you need to eat half of my rations to keep your strength up."

More open badland stretched in front of them, stitched with smaller crevies and full of high, rolling dunes that made them pitch and yaw so much that Lillam began to feel queasy. It didn't help that Doaks coaxed a little more velocity from the freshly charged wagon as they drove through the rough landscape. A sense of terrible urgency had descended upon them since listening to the Prophet's last proclamation, one that made Rand so jittery he couldn't think about much else. So, after making breakfast and distributing water rations, he huddled around the small table where Korden and Meech drew rounds of totala, hoping to take his mind away from the anxiety.

"Deal me in?" he asked.

Meech raised an eyebrow. "You remember how to play?"

"Oh please, let me show you youngsters a thing or two…"

But, two hours later, the boy was whipping them both on every front. While Meech shuffled cards for a new hand, Rand said, "I've never seen anyone stave off two hard charges without sacrificing their Miser. Where'd you learn to play like that?"

Korden looked pleased as he answered, "Several of my teachers loved to play. We had tournaments. Then they stopped being able to win against me."

Rand frowned thoughtfully. "You mentioned these 'teachers' before. What did they teach you? Besides a brutal totala hand, I mean."

"Everything, really. History, math, literature. And art-craft, of course."

"Oh." Rand couldn't help glancing toward Lillam at the mention of the uncomfortable subject, but she appeared to be napping. "And these teachers, they're the ones who raised you?"

"Yes. Them and my...my father."

The boy's pause wasn't lost on Rand. He gave a sympathetic nod as Meech dealt fresh towers. "And where is he now? Did he toss you out on the side of the road and run too, like ours did?"

Korden picked up his cards and studied them intently as he said, "Incarnates killed him. Nearly a season ago."

Meech gasped. "Li'l drude...I didn't know." He glared at Rand. "Why don't you jam that foot even deeper in your mouth, brother?"

"I-I'm sorry, I shouldn't have pried," Rand sputtered.

"It's all right," Korden assured him. His voice took on a hard undercurrent as he said, "Truth be told, he wasn't *really* my father. His name was Redfen. I suppose I don't even know his real last name. He was just...a man who ran with me when I was a baby."

"A Rearing," Rand translated. Korden gave him a questioning frown. "That's what the Saint-of-Christers call it when someone goes nomadic with a child to keep them away from the Incarnates. It's supposed to be a...a very noble undertaking."

"So that's what you and Lillam are doing now?"

"We took a bit of an early start, but yes, essentially. Although I hope our running will come to an end when we make it to the Skyreach." Eager to make up for his blunder, Rand said, "I'm sure this man—Redfen—must've held a lot of love for you to go on a Rearing. It's more than our parents did for us."

"Hey, that's not fair, man." Meech sounded stung. "They kept us alive as long as they could."

"Oh, they did, huh? Eleven years was the extent of their abilities?"

"Maybe it was."

"Then they shouldn't've had a second kid."

Meech's face twitched with aggravation, but he said to Korden, "We're not sure what was goin through their heads when they left us. Maybe they were sick and knew they wouldn't be around much longer. Or maybe they wanted to teach us to take care of ourselves. Maybe they were scouting ahead and planned on coming back, but something happened."

Rand groaned. "Curse, if I'd known you were going to cling to those fairy stories your whole life, I never would've told them to you in the first place." It was an old argument between them, but this time, frustration made him go a step further. "Face it, once they left us, their next stop was probably the closest tavern to celebrate. That is, if Dad didn't sell Mom to a cronehouse first."

Meech slapped his cards down on the table. "Don't talk about them like that! Just because you don't want your child, doesn't mean the same about them!"

Again, Rand's head whipped over to Lillam's sleeping form before he answered. "What makes you think I don't want my child?"

"C'mon, Rand. I'm spun, not dumb." Meech's grin was taunting. "Do you mean to claim *this* is what you wanted? To be rattling across the desert with me, hunted by Incarnates for the second time in your life, 'steada back in Ida sucklin at Hildan's teat?"

Rand stood up, knocking over the whole table in the

process. "Don't think you know me, you worthless jinkoid crumb! I gave up *everything* to be here!"

"Oh sure, yes, give my brother the biiiiig prize for his sacrifice! Which I'm sure we'll be hearin about for years to come, the same way you remind me every day about the *noble Rearing* you went on for me!" Meech rose as well, meeting him eye-to-eye. It struck Rand how improved his brother appeared after this last week in the desert away from his drug, less pale, putting on weight, the puckered scars on his arms healing up. "But here's the real question: would you've gotten involved with her in the first place, if you knew it'd come to this?" He shook his head slowly, as though answering the question for Rand. "Lie to yourself all you want, but know this: you wouldn't be the first drude in history to regret shootin his seed into fertile soil."

Rand's hands curled into fists at his sides. Meech did the same. The two of them had come to blows many times in their youth, but this felt different, like years of pent-up resentment and unspoken recriminations coming to a head. Before the fight could get under way, the wagon gave a hard lurch beneath their feet that sent them both crashing into one of the cabinets. Lillam yelped as she rolled out of their nest in the corner. Their speed jumped up even more, turning the stale breeze blowing through the middle of the vehicle into a whistling gale that scattered their totala deck across the bonnet. Forgetting about the fight, Rand headed toward the control deck with Korden right behind him.

"*What's the matter?*" he asked their driver over the screech of the wind.

"*That is!*" Doaks jerked his head to the right. Rand

turned in that direction and saw that the entire horizon to the east was embroiled with angry brown clouds.

"Aged Lord help us," he uttered.

"*Maelstrom!*" Doaks explained. He furiously worked the controls, swerving around the steeper dunes to keep the wagon pointed toward another group of mesas a few spans away. "*We gotta make it to cover or the damn thing'll bury us! I recommend yah batten down the hatches in there!*"

They spent the next few minutes securing everything they could in cabinets and closing both bonnet doors, so the interior quickly became sweltering. Doaks faded the walls so they could see their progress, but it became apparent they wouldn't reach the plateaus before the storm bore down on them. Rand watched the billowing mass approach, blackening the sky. It looked like a solid wall of sand rushing toward them, with stuttering flashes of lightning at its heart. The air pressure preceding the maelstrom was so great, the dunes rippled away from it, moving outward like ocean waves. A low rumble built in the air that they could feel even over the thrum of the engine.

"*We ain't stoppin!*" Doaks shouted over the wagon's speakers as he pulled a pair of goggles over his eyes and then hurried to buckle a strap across his lap. "*Yah better hold on to somethin, this could get rough!*"

The idea came to Rand in a clear burst. He retrieved the long coil of hempen rope from the cabinet and began cutting off lengths. "*Tie yourselves to something! Around the waist, if you can!*"

Korden slid beneath the cot at the front of the bonnet and worked on securing himself to it. They could hear his panicked, wheezing breaths even over the approaching grumble of the sandstorm. Rand helped Lillam attach her upper chest to the solid metal pipes running into the back of the cold storage cases and then wedged himself in beside her before telling his brother, "*Meech, hurry up!*"

"*I don't need your frammin help!*" Meech sat on the floor, arms stubbornly crossed.

"*Zeega!*" Korden shouted, scrambling to untie himself. They all looked up through the invisible roof, where the stoic purple and black creature perched, oblivious (or perhaps just uncaring) of the danger. "*We have to get her inside!*"

"*Stop!*" Rand told him. "*There's no time!*"

As if to spite him, Meech scrambled to his feet. "*I'll get her!*"

In the next instant, the maelstrom swept over them.

They dropped into a dark, howling void. Shrieking wind buffeted the sides of the wagon, shoving it over to a precipitous angle before rocking it back as far in the other direction. That cushion of light which made their ride so smooth regardless of the terrain was now an unsteady base allowing them to bob like a raft on a tempestuous sea. Rand heard objects crashing in the cabinets and Lillam screaming in his ear and a deep, groaning squall from below as some part of the craft dragged against the ground. During one dazzling barrage of lightning, he saw Meech roll past him, tossed by the bucking floor.

Without thinking, Rand let go of Lillam and leaned forward to snatch at his brother. Their hands found one another as the deck pitched, throwing them both across the vehicle. The base of the sink slammed into Rand's stomach.

He lay on the ground and wrapped his arms around it while Meech clung to his waist.

"*Doaks!*" he cried out when his breath returned, hoping the man could hear him through the wagon's speakers. With the bonnet transparent, he could see their driver had switched on the vehicle's headlights. The twin cones of illumination couldn't reach more than ten pargs ahead in the driving sheets of sand. "*Are we almost there?*"

The other man didn't respond. He was wrestling to keep the wagon from slewing side to side.

Which was why Rand saw the half-buried boulder loom out of the storm before Doaks did.

"*Watch out!*" he yelled.

Even if their driver had heard the warning, he wouldn't have been fast enough to react. One side of the vehicle scraped across the boulder and then bounced upward as the hover engines tried to compensate. The wagon tilted violently, launching into a brief spiral before crashing over onto its side and rolling through the sand.

Rand heard a deep tearing sound from the polymer bonnet, before Gwenita spit him into the storm.

2

Lillam wasn't sure how she ended up outside. One second she'd been holding on for dear life while Gwenita shook to pieces around her. The next, she was sitting on the ground amid the raging sandstorm, with pain radiating across her chest from her wounded shoulder.

She looked around dazedly, squinting her eyes against

the harsh wind. The world was nothing but a brown blur around her, full of stinging particles. Then, during a burst of lightning, she spotted a hulking shadow fifteen pargs away to her left; it took her a moment to recognize the wagon lying on its side, the bonnet crushed in. Just beyond it, the towering column of a mesa climbed toward the dark sky.

Rand, her mind whispered, sending a flutter of panic into her limbs.

Lillam stood, ignoring the head rush that almost sent her reeling back to her knees. The wind came from every direction at once, snatching at her hair, tearing at the oversized tunic she wore. She pushed through it toward the wagon, following a trail of wreckage that littered the ground, most of it already half-buried. The vehicle doors— now sideways—were sealed, but the faux-canvas bonnet had a huge hole in it, revealing the arched support struts, like a ribcage made of polymer. She ducked inside, out of the wind, and gazed around the canted interior.

Debris was strewn everywhere: clothing, food stores, bits of machinery. A few of the trunks and cabinets had come loose from the walls. She sifted through it all frantically, searching for Rand, the one person that kept her going through these miserable days, but there didn't appear to be anyone inside. A frustrated sob escaped her, gobbled up immediately by the storm. How had this ruination come upon them so fast, without warning? Lillam was on the verge of leaving when she spotted an arm sticking out from an overturned cabinet. She grabbed hold and pulled with all her might.

The boy slid out from under the obstruction and lay unmoving at her feet.

Lillam gasped and recoiled. She'd touched him, touched his bare, filthy, Crafter flesh. Lillam started to move away, but guilt jabbed at her. She forced herself to come back and leaned over to check him.

He wasn't breathing.

She recalled his labored inhalations before the storm hit, and something she'd overheard him telling Meech a few days ago, about his lung affliction. Lillam knelt, patted his cheeks, pressed on his chest. Nothing.

Leave him, then. Go and find Rand.

The boy's words came back to her, about thinking she was brave. And Rand's insistence that their lives were in his hands.

Working on instinct, Lillam steeled herself, bent down, fastened her lips onto his, and blew into his mouth as hard as she could.

There was a shudder deep in his chest, then he was coughing against her. She broke contact, sputtering, as ragged, wheezing gasps worked in and out of his lungs. His eyes remained closed though; whatever she'd done had jumpstarted his breathing, but not brought him back to consciousness. She got to her feet, wrapped an arm around his narrow chest, and hoisted him off the ground. He was surprising light, but the weight still taxed her as she dragged him from the wagon.

A hand fell on her injured shoulder when she stepped back into the wind. Doaks loomed out of the storm beside her, goggles over his eyes and the lower half of his face covered in blood that crusted over with sand as fast as it could gush from his nostrils. He took the boy's bulk from her, draping the unconscious form over his own squat shoulders, and gestured toward the mesa. "*That way!*"

"*Where's Rand?*"

"*I ain't seen him or his brother!*" Doaks latched on to her wrist and pulled her forward. "*C'mon, let's get to shelter!*"

"*No!*" She jerked free of his grip. "*I have to find him!*"

The man pointed again at the bluff. "*That's the sole reason we ain't already dead! It's blockin the worst of the wind! Yah go beyond it, this storm'll sand yah down to nuthin! If he's out there, it's too late for him!*"

Lillam put a hand to her stomach. The life inside her must come first. *Rand*, she thought. *I'm so sorry.*

She lurched into motion, running ahead of Doaks toward the refuge of the mesa. But she'd taken only a few steps before the sand rose up to grab at her feet. Lillam looked down, watched as the ground gobbled her legs up, and then she was sinking into a crushing oblivion.

3

The humans needn't have worried about the storm bothering Zeega (she'd seen far worse weather in the deadly *hoshnitath* breeding farms), but when the wagon crashed, she was launched from the roof like a *crigish* taking flight. The force of the ejection would've killed most beings, but she tucked herself into a tight ball and rolled fifty pargs across the sand before smashing into a boulder near the base of the plateau. The spongy bag of her flesh tore in several places and one foreclaw felt disjointed, but she ignored the injuries and raced back into the storm, following Korden's mental scent. She reached him in time to see the female named Lillam get sucked down into the ground.

Doaks, that deplorable human who'd cut off her appendage, stood nearby, with an unconscious Korden draped over his back. "*What happened to her?*" Zeega demanded, her voice shrill.

"*Suck sand!*" he answered. "*She's gone!*"

Unfortunately, he is right, the disembodied one told her from his cradle on Korden's neck. I calculate a .08 percent chance of survival.

Zeega stared at the place where the female had plunged into the ground. Her panicked thoughts were audible from somewhere below the surface. She was babbling in her own head as she asphyxiated.

And yet, most of her concern was for the life inside her, rather than her own.

The overturned wagon sat a few steps farther. Zeega scuttled into it and returned dragging the rest of the hempen rope that Doaks had traded his wares for. She dropped the coil at his feet and then climbed his body. Doaks balked and tried to knock her away, but she continued upward until her tentacles could knot around his neck.

"*When Zeega tugs on this rope, you will pull it back up,*" she snarled in his bloody face, "*otherwise she will rise from this pit and snip off all of your fingers and toes before ripping out your throat.*"

Zeega didn't have time to gauge how well the threat worked. She grabbed one end of the cord with her functional foreclaw and dove into the sinkhole.

4

After he fell out of the wagon, Rand careened down the slope of a long dune, unable to slow his fall. Every time he found a handhold in the sand, it eroded beneath his fingers. On and on he tumbled, into the dark gullet of the storm.

An unknowable amount of time later, he somersaulted head over heels and came to rest on a level stretch of ground. Rand had just enough time to sit up before another body bowled him right back over, and then his brother was lying on top of him. They untangled themselves and helped one another up.

The maelstrom raged around them, so violent they could feel it all the way to their bones. Rand never imagined anything in the world could be capable of such chaotic fury. Within seconds, the shifting dunes had piled up around their feet, burying them up to the calf. Sand stung Rand's exposed skin, abrading his flesh raw, and every breath he took was full of more grit than air. He coughed and gagged, then lifted his tunic up over his mouth and nose. The filter helped, but not much.

Meech grabbed his shoulders, trying to tell him something, but the words were drowned out by the screeching gales. Rand leaned closer until his brother's mouth was next to his ear.

"*We're gonna die out here!*"

No. Rand refused to believe that. He wouldn't let himself die before he could be sure Lillam was safe. "*We need to keep moving and find the wagon!*"

"*How? I can't see a damn thing!*"

Rand couldn't either. His own hand was lost when he extended his arm, and it was impossible to keep his eyes open longer than a second or two before the wind forced them back closed. Already he'd gotten so turned around, he couldn't even say for sure which dune they'd fallen down. Getting lost in this storm would surely mean their death. He swiveled his head anyway, straining to catch a glimpse of something while the sand scraped and clawed at him.

Lillam, he thought. *Where are you?*

And then, suddenly, he *could* see. Something, anyway. A little above and to his right, a shimmering glow shone through the veil of the storm.

No, not just one glow, but several distinct flares in varying shades of dirty yellow and serene blue and vivid red, shaped in the vague outlines of people. He could clearly make out the yellow and red forms moving, with the blue slumped over on top of the latter.

Even stranger, he could somehow see them when he squeezed his eyes shut, ghostly candle flames in the darkness behind his lids that stayed fixed in the same location.

"*I'm sorry*," Meech blubbered beside him. "*I didn't mean what I said, man, you'll be a great father, and—!*"

"*Hush on!*" Rand grabbed his brother's head and pointed it toward the glows. "*Do you see that light?*"

"*I told you, I don't see anything!*"

"*C'mon, I'll lead you!*"

Rand took his brother's hand and worked his way up the side of the dune.

5

Sand forced its way into Lillam's nose and down her throat. Intense pressure on her chest squeezed out the last bit of air left inside her. She couldn't move, not so much as a finger, but she could still feel herself sinking, the sand shifting and moving as though eager to draw her into its ruthless embrace.

I tried, she told her daughter. In that moment, she was glad they hadn't taken the time to think up a name for the child; it would've made saying goodbye that much worse. *I tried so hard, but I couldn't protect you from this world.*

Even through her growing panic, she registered an odd movement under her feet, a sense of something firm. At first, she thought she'd reached the bottom of this cruel pit, touched down on some bedrock where she would rot forever, but this was more like gentle hands that halted her downward journey.

And then they were all around her, encircling her arms and waist.

The pressure on her eased. The packed sand loosened. Instead of sinking deeper, those strange hands reversed her direction, passing her back up toward precious air. It just wasn't happening fast enough.

Lillam's consciousness flickered out as a tentacle found her wrist.

6

As long as she succumbed to gravity, Zeega had an easy time maneuvering through the grit. By bunching and rippling the muscles in her many tentacles, she could make the soil flow around her, hastening her descent into the sinkhole. Blind and deaf amid the incredible compression, she used her mental senses to guide her toward the human female, whose thoughts were fading fast.

It was only as she reached Lillam that she discovered there was another entity nearby. Zeega detected the same intangible presence she'd sensed with Korden in the desert. Its emotional aura was gossamer and inconstant—a polychromatic prism so nuanced and ceaselessly shifting, it was impossible to decipher—but she could read its exertion as it ensnared the female and tried to reverse her fall.

Body crying out for air, Zeega worked her way around the female's back and under her arms, tying a quick loop with the rope. That ghostly presence swirled around her as she worked, holding Lillam in place somehow. When Zeega finished, she gave the line a hard tug and then held on as they were hauled parg by parg toward the surface.

7

"No, it wasn't a person at all," Lillam insisted. "It was like…like the sand came to life around me…"

The storm ended as quickly as it began, the afternoon sky lightening from black to hazy orange in a matter of seconds. They'd spent the next hour gathering up as many of their belongings as they could reclaim from the desert while Korden righted the wagon so Doaks could assess the damage. They'd lost a battery and one of the three talkies in the crash, along with some food, clothing, and personal items. Now they gathered in the long shade of the mesa, far away from any sand spires, to recount their stories in full.

Rand pulled Lillam closer. The pair hadn't stopped touching since their reunion amid the maelstrom, after they'd revived her. But his words held a playfully disbelieving lilt as he said, "Sweetlove, you were drowning in suck sand. Your perceptions can't exactly be trusted."

"Zeega sensed the entity as well." The riftling hunkered on the ground beside Korden, nursing one of her foreclaws. She turned her eyes up to him and added, "It was the same shifting *mohol* as the previous night. And it appeared to be helping."

"Then I owe it as much gratitude as I owe you." Lillam leaned over and held out a hand to Zeega. She pulled away, wide mouth drawing back in an expression somewhere between a frown and a grimace, but then she submitted and allowed the woman to briefly caress her side. "You saved my life, Zeega."

"Yes," Rand agreed. "And I never thanked you for saving mine when I was dangling off the back of the wagon. You came out of the woods and crashed those other hovering vehicles, otherwise I'd surely be dead."

"Zeega does not require gratitude," she mumbled. But Korden detected the slightest hint of pleasure beneath the claim.

He turned to Lillam. "And I suppose I have to say the same to you, for restarting my lungs."

She waved off the acknowledgment also. "It's a miracle none of us were killed in the crash." She picked up Rand's hand and stroked his raw knuckles, where the sandstorm had stripped away the flesh. "And that you were both able to find us in the storm."

"That was all Rand," Meech told them from where he lay sprawled across the ground. "If he hadn't seen those lights, we'da been sanded down to the bone in a few more minutes."

"Lights?" Korden asked.

"Yeah, drude! He kept goin on about how you guys were glowin and he could see you through the sand!"

"I was probably hallucinating," Rand said, but his aura revealed that he wasn't entirely convinced of his own assertion. "We just got lucky I took us in the right direction, that's all."

Doaks came around the rocky corner of the plateau then, wiping sweat and sand from his brow. His nose was badly broken, lying squashed in the middle of his face like a rotten potato.

"Is she working?" Korden asked.

"Yes sah!" Doaks answered cheerfully. "Engines intakes were clogged, but once I got the sand cleared out, she fired right up! Freezers came back online and one of the batteries is even in good shape. Old girl's sure not much to look at anymore, but I think she could get us where we're goin."

"That's fantastic news!" Rand exclaimed.

Doaks beamed. "Sure is! Too bad we're gonna die anyway!"

The others frowned at each other, his jolly tone making them believe they'd misheard.

"What do you mean?" Korden asked. The man's *mohol* seethed with anger and regret. "I thought you said she could get us where we're going."

"Oh ayuh, she sure could! But *we* won't make it that far!" The huge grin was still in place, but it looked morbid beneath his swollen nose as he spread his arms and declared, "Because the crash cracked the water tank, rubos! Every last drop of liquid we had is gone! And in a couple of days, that sun is gonna dry us out like burnt toast!"

Tuscarora

THE GREATEST GIFT

1

They strung blankets across the hole in the wagon's bonnet, giving them back some measure of shade. Gwenita's walls would never again turn invisible, and most of the 'DOC APOCALYPSE' lettering on the outside had been scraped away by the wind and sand. Once Doaks dropped the sarcastic happiness routine, his displeasure about the damage was clear. As they got moving without any water, Rand heard him mutter to Korden, "I guess we'll see how well yah Upper provides after all…"

In their current predicament, reaching the Prophet—and any help he might be able to offer—was their best bet. Doaks figured they were another week and a half away from the eastern edge of the Valley versus five to six days from the Prophet's location to the north, so they just needed to figure a way to survive that long. But, by the time they stopped, as the last feeble splash of sunset sank the dunes into an ocean of shadows, thirst was already a niggling annoyance in the back of Rand's throat. They ate supper around a crackling fire, sucking the juice out of several thick-skinned jiccamelons thawed out from the depths of the freezer. Then Doaks ventured into the darkness to hunt for night-blooming dasher blossoms from which to extract moisture, taking Meech with him so he could train someone else in the process. Lillam stumbled to bed soon after, and Zeega climbed back to her roost atop the wagon, leaving Korden and Rand alone beside the fire.

The boy studied him across the glowing embers without speaking for a long time. When his gaze began to make Rand uncomfortable, he asked, "What? What is it?"

"These lights you saw during the storm. Can you describe them?"

Rand frowned. "They were…colorful hazes that out-lined your bodies. Like I said, I was hallucinating." He gave a laugh that came out sounding a bit frazzled. "I could see them with my eyes closed, so they couldn't have been real."

The kid whispered something that sounded like 'moles.'

"What did you say?"

"Auras," Korden elaborated, as if that made it any clearer. "You were seeing *auras*. Was that the first time they ever appeared to you?"

"'Auras?' I'm sorry, I don't understand what you're talking about."

"They're an emotional spectrum. A way of sensing another being's feelings. Only Crafters can see them."

Rand stiffened. "I'm not a Crafter."

But Korden was sitting forward eagerly. "The bullet outside Ida. The one that almost hit me when the Incarnates were firing at us. With everything else that happened right after, I forgot all about it." His mouth fell open as he looked at Rand. "*You* stopped it. With artcraft."

"No. That is not true." That invigorating tingle was back, buzzing through Rand's skull, making the short hair along the back of his neck stand up.

"But this is great!" Korden insisted, voice high with excitement. "I've never met anyone else so young that could—!"

Rand leapt at him, boots scattering ash from the fire in his haste to get to the boy. He seized Korden by the front of his tunic and yanked him up.

"*Shut your framming mouth*," he hissed through his teeth. "I don't care what you think you saw, I am *not* a Crafter. And if you ever say that I am, to *anybody*, you and I will be enemies. Is that clear?"

The boy's face crumpled. He nodded.

Rand let go of him and walked away as an eel made of shame writhed in the pit of his stomach.

2

Doaks and Meech returned after several hours with a bladder of sour, milky fluid that made Korden think of leather oil, but they were all too thirsty to complain about the flavor. Divvied up, it amounted to little more than a sip each, a dash of perfunctory relief on their feverish tongues that was forgotten almost immediately. When morning rolled around (following a night of dreamless sleep, thanks to Zeega), Korden's whole body ached and his throat felt coated in sand. Even worse, the conversation with Rand from the night before haunted his thoughts before his eyes even opened, the thrill of finding another Crafter and Rand's violent rejection of the discovery. But Stone's urgent entreaty for him to listen to the most recent broadcast from the Prophet made him forget all about physical and mental discomforts. Korden might've kept this new message to himself, but since the others had found out he could play them for the group, they demanded to hear every update as soon as it was available.

"Um...hi," the broadcast began. The Prophet's upbeat tone and baffling word choices were gone, replaced with apprehension. "Today, I'm speaking directly to the people aboard the hovering vehicle in the Great Basin Desert. Because you can hear me...can't you? Yes, I think there's little doubt about that anymore. To be honest, I've never actually known if anyone was listening, so I just kept shouting into the void, hoping that *some*one, *some*where was getting use out of my blabbering." He gave a tired chuckle. "And you're not just hearing me, either. You know where I am. Accounting for every deviation in the landscape, your trajectory continues to point you exactly in my direction. And to that, I must say...*do not come here.*" The command was forceful, perhaps even a bit angry. "I don't know who you are or what business you think you have with me, but change your course, pilgrims. Under other circumstances, I'd love to meet you, but the way things are looking, you'd arrive here wearing that Incarnate army like a tail, and, I'm sorry, I can't have you bringing your troubles to my doorstep. I am happy to continue giving you updates on their progress, but I will make no further broadcasts until I see you're complying with my request. This is the

Weatherman, signing off."

"So that's it." Rand hunkered on the other end of the battered bonnet, as far from Korden as he could get. "We go east and head for the end of the Valley."

"Without water, we'll be dead 'fore we get within three hundred spans of the edge," Doaks told him matter-of-factly.

"We don't have to go without water," Rand pointed out. He kept his eyes rooted on the ground as he added, "Not if Korden magics some up."

Meech bolted up with hands fisted. "He already told you he can't! Whatever he conjures could kill us all!"

"If we're going to die anyway, we might as well take the chance."

"He's right," Korden said. "I've got to at least try."

Lillam said quietly, "This is what we deserve. For leaving those men behind." Rand put a hand on her shoulder, but she shrugged it off. "'Eat what you grow,' that's what the Aged Lord says."

"Be that as it may…" Doaks crossed his hairy arms and scowled around at them. "If the kid don't know for sure that he can help us, then this Prophet is still our only chance for survival. We should go to 'im and see if we can convince 'im to help us."

"And if he doesn't?" Meech asked.

A hard glint came into Doaks's eyes above his broken nose, the same one that had been there whenever he'd shocked Korden to make him obey. His aura pulsed with treacherous silver as he said, "Well then rubos, the question becomes…how bad do you wanna live?"

3

Another grueling day of travel passed, and, though the most tiresome activity he'd undertaken was fanning himself and Lillam to keep the heat at bay, Rand's muscles felt like raw bread dough. The dehydration made him irritable and weak, and the others were faring just as poorly. Lillam, in particular, complained of a severe headache and stayed curled into a ball in their corner. When he asked her for the third time if she thought the baby would be all right, she barked, "How should I know, I've never even *seen* anyone who was pregnant!"

Korden tried three times to conjure water from thin air, concentrating hard with an old polymer bucket on the deck in front of him. One second, the vessel would be empty, and the next, filled to the brim with liquid, an effect that seemed false to the eye, like the wavery mirages they could see in the distance all around them. The boy allowed no one else to touch these concoctions, just swirled some in his mouth until his computer could perform an analysis. Two of the attempts turned out cloudy blue and unfit for consumption. The third was so clear it made Rand ache just looking at it, but the fluid had crystalline shards suspended in it that resembled ice and burned the kid's lips before he could even taste it.

They all perked up once the sun went down and the cooler night air blew in; the temperatures after dark might not be any more pleasant, but the cold wouldn't dehydrate them as fast as the heat. There was plenty to eat for dinner, except each bite tasted bitter and interminably chewy to Rand without something to wash it down his dry throat.

When they finished, Doaks stood up and announced, "More of us'll need to go out dasher draining tonight, so we can cover more ground. Meech, yah take the kid and show him how it's done. Your brother'll come with me. Tomorrow night all of us can scatter around."

Rand didn't bother to hide his relief at the suggestion. The last thing he wanted was to be alone around the campfire with Korden, whom he hadn't spoken to all day.

He made sure Lillam was settled with a talkie in case she needed him, then followed Doaks into the wasteland.

They were barely out of sight of the wagon before the other man said, "All right, I admit, I had a bit of an ulterior motive for bringin yah out here."

Rand put his palms to his cheeks in mock surprise. "You? Ulterior motive? I don't believe it."

Doaks grinned and held up his hand. "I just wanna chat."

"We have nothing to 'chat' about."

Rand continued plodding through the sand, but Doaks hurried to stand in his path. "Wait on now, just wait on a tick! I know we got our diff'rences, but, on the whole, yah seem like yah might be a touch more reasonable than the resta that rabble."

Coming from this man, Rand did *not* take it as a compliment. But he was too tired and thirsty and cold to argue. "What do you want?" he asked warily.

Doaks tugged at his beard as though hesitant, but the action appeared calculated to Rand. "We *do* have another play here, friend," he said. "The Prophet or Weatherman or whatever he calls hisself…he said he'd be glad to meet us if we didn't have every demon for ten-thousand spans crawlin up our ass cheeks. And the only reason *they're* chasin us is the boy. So maybe if we show up there without 'im…"

"You son of a crone. If you think I'll help you hurt him—"

"*Hurt* 'im? Nobody said anything about hurtin 'im!" Doaks looked horrified, but again, Rand was acutely aware that the man made a living telling people exactly what they needed to hear. "Kid's gotten so powerful, I don't think we *could* hurt 'im. No, I'm talkin about…yah know…leavin him somewhere while we go beg the Prophet for enough water to get outta this cursey desert!"

Rand waved a hand around at the desolate landscape. "You don't think abandoning him out here would hurt him?"

"Least it'd give 'im a chance. Us too."

"And I'm sure it'd be an unintended boon that we also wouldn't be anywhere near him if the Incarnates catch up."

"What if it is?" Doaks growled, all pretense and composure vanishing. "We stood by the boy, did everything we could for 'im, but this is a losin battle! Even if we somehow keep from shrivelin up like salted snails, that army's gonna overrun us eventually! And I don't relish the idea of havin my guts ripped out by a packa rotheads! Cause that's what they'll do to *all* of us, includin what's inside that preggers filly of yahs!"

"They don't kill the unborn."

"No, they don't *hunt* the unborn. Cause they can't sense 'em till they pop out. But slaughterin a fetal teatsucker when they get the chance sure saves 'em some problems down the line."

Rand took a deep breath that dragged through his parched throat. "Then maybe we should talk to him, convince him to wait somewhere while we—"

Doaks shook his head. "The kid is completely irrational, yah've seen 'im. Can't afford to tip our hand in case he disagrees. Best thing to do is steal away in the night, leave him and his little black squid in our wake. If we get the water—and there's time—we'll come back for 'em."

"But what if we need his magic?"

The other man was silent as his eyes flicked back and forth in deliberation. Then he leaned closer to Rand and lowered his voice to ask, "Why would we need him...when we got *yah*?"

Rand's heart rocketed into his throat. "What do you mean?"

"Didn't say anything before cause yah seemed kinda mum about it, but..." He winked and laid a finger aside one swollen nostril. "I saw yah leanin off the side of Gwenita that day."

"Th-that, that...that was nothing," Rand stammered.

"Oh, ayuh, I'm sure all bureaucratic rule-pushers are acrobats in their spare time. C'mon rubo, I recognize magic when I see it. Least, I do now."

"I am not a Crafter," Rand said, his second such denial in two days.

"Crafter, warlock, spellflinger; I don't care what yah call it, yah got *power*! Power that could help get us outta this mess in ways the boy refuses to!"

"I...but I can't..."

"Look, just think on it, but think fast. In the meantime, let's milk some dasher blossoms."

4

Doaks ran him through the process, how to forage for the slightly luminescent ground buds and extract moisture from them using a knife and bladder, then they split up to search parallel dunes. Rand tried to put the man's proposal—and his assertions—out of his mind as he worked, but it wasn't easy.

He was not a Crafter; that much he knew. To prove this, he stopped his hunt several times, concentrated, and tried to duplicate any of the many wonders of which Korden was capable. To conjure fire or wood or make even a single grain of sand move.

But nothing happened, not even that tingle beneath his scalp, the one that made him feel as if he could count the stars themselves.

Rand spotted a faint glow in the sand to his left while the argument raged in his mind. As he approached, it resolved into not one, but two rounded bulbs, growing side by side. Rand knelt in front of them, noting how the illumination glowed greener than the other yellowish plants, and how the centers resembled pupils with—

The sand rippled and erupted in front of him as a huge, lumbering shape burst up from the ground. Rand glimpsed a long, low body before he was bowled over onto his back. Leathery paws twice the size of his hands seized his chest and began spinning him roughly down the dune, flipping his body over and over like a flapjack on the griddle. He screamed around a mouthful of sand.

Doaks's voice came from somewhere above him. "Oh fram, that's a scorpigator! It's deathrollin yah!"

"*Help me!*" Rand squealed. The creature above him felt heavy and strong enough to rend him apart, yet it continued tumbling him through the sand so fast it was difficult to draw a breath. And those he did catch were filled with a nauseating musk that reminded him of overspiced food.

"Sorry!" Doaks returned, his voice already fading. "Not much I can do about that! But I'll tell 'em yah died savin me!"

Rand wanted to bellow an insult, but the words were smothered out of him. The violent spinning motion was making him ill. His thoughts filled with images of Lillam, and how he would give anything to see her again.

Then craft! his mind told him madly. *You did it before, you* know *you did! So imagine it or make a wish or however the hells it happened!*

Then I wish this thing would...would get swallowed up by suck sand!

Something pulsed inside his mind as he pictured exactly what the scene would look like, a pleasant sensation not unlike the spasm at the end his and Lillam's lovemaking. The heavy paws on his torso lifted away. Rand slid to a stop in the sand and sat up with his head reeling.

He could see the scorpigator clearly in the moonlight now, just pargs away. As its name implied, it had the scaly body of a swamp lizard—albeit with two extra legs in the middle—but a narrow tail attached to its rear end curved up and back over the long torso. An oblong, insectile head sat on the front, with those two glowing eyes situated above a pyramidal beak. The creature was twice his size, and right now it was struggling to pull its back four legs out of a vortex in the sand beneath it. Every attempt to wriggle free made it sink a few cupits deeper.

I did that, Rand thought in disbelief.

The beast fixed its intended meal with those green eyes as it thrashed in the suck sand. A half-parg long stinger emerged from the tip of its arched tail. The appendage reared back and whipped at him.

Without being conscious of what he was doing, Rand pushed outward, not with his hands but with his *mind*.

A shimmering green cloud leapt out of him, expanding from the center of his forehead. The stinger was swatted aside by this wave before it could strike him, the impact so hard that something in the tail snapped. The last third of the appendage hung limp at an awkward angle as it withdrew.

That pyramid on the front of the scorpigator's face opened, splitting into four segmented jaws that revealed a long gullet lined with fangs. A frustrated, ululating cry issued from within as it surged forward in one last desperate attempt to bite him in half.

In the split second it took for the scorpigator's jaws to reach him, an image formed in Rand's head: those smooth cobblestones that made up Ida's streets, the ultimate representation of peace and safety for him. He pictured one of them clearly, yearned for its existence as he'd never yearned for anything before.

An object appeared in the middle of the creature's gaping mouth, popping into existence as the imperfect water had appeared in the bucket in front of Korden. Superficially, it *resembled* the stone bricks from his home—the same texture and shape—but it was lime green and uneven in structure, a crude caricature. Whatever it was, it became wedged so deeply in the beast's jaws that they couldn't close on him. The scorpigator reared back and shook its buggish head, trying to dislodge the obstruction even as it slid deeper into the sinkhole.

Rand scrambled out of its reach before it could try again. He got to his feet and ran.

He caught up with Doaks outside their camp. The man looked shocked to see him but recovered quickly. "Good, yah got free! Used that magic, did yah? I figured I'd get help and—"

Rand shoved him to the ground.

"We're all expendable to you, aren't we?" he asked. "As long as you come out on top, that's all that matters. And that's why no one will ever be on your side."

He left the man blubbering more excuses and hurried on to the wagon.

5

Korden was bone-weary by the time he and Meech returned to camp, with a quarter-full bladder of moisture to show for their efforts. As bad as he wanted to guzzle it (and despite Stone's dire warning that catastrophic organ failure was only three days away), they decided to wait for morning. Meech stumbled off toward his bedroll, but, when Korden arrived at his own spot beneath the rear deck of the wagon, he found Rand waiting for him, his aura a bubbling cauldron of angst.

"How?" the man demanded without preamble. "How did I get like this? Why all of a sudden, when *you* came into my life? Is Lillam right, did you infect me somehow?"

Korden fought through his surprise to shake his head. "It doesn't work like that."

"Then how does it work? I've never done anything like this before. So why can I do it now?"

"Because...because you made it happen," he said, reaching for an explanation the man would accept. "Because some part of you *needed* it, like you never have before."

"Bullcurse. You think I couldn't've used some magic when I was left alone at the age of eleven to keep myself and my brother safe from the Incarnates?"

Korden held up his hands in the face of Rand's frustration. "I don't have all the answers. I can only tell you that Crafting is a granted ability, but it requires imagination to fuel it, willpower to use it, and, most importantly, faith to sustain it."

"Faith? Faith in *what*?"

"Well...the Upper."

"*But I don't even know what that is!*" Rand shouted in a rough whisper, hands fisted at this sides. "*So how can I have faith in it?*"

That was the pertinent question, the one Korden most needed to reconcile, not just for Rand, but for himself. "Maybe...somewhere deep in your heart...you *do* believe. You just don't accept it yet."

"Of course, that makes a lot of sense." Rand gave a slow, derisive chuckle that sounded like a whimper. He slumped over the edge of the deck. "I don't need this complication in my life."

Korden's own anger surfaced. "It's not a complication. It's a gift. The greatest you could ever receive."

"Well, I don't want it." The rejection made Korden think of his last conversation with Tash before he left the village, as he tried to deny the path the Upper had set him upon. "Can't you show me how to…I don't know…switch it off?"

Korden eased up to the wagon beside him. "Would you mind if I tried something?"

Rand lifted one shoulder in defeat. Korden reached over and took hold of the sides of his head, gently forcing the man to face him, then placed his thumbs over the eyelids to keep them closed. He'd never attempted anything like this, never been trained to enter minds, but he remembered the recording Stone played for him back in their earliest time on the road together, an accounting by a journalist who'd spoken to an elderly Crafter in the last days of the old world.

Korden closed his own eyes, reaching out for Rand's *mohol*. His head flinched in Korden's hands when the connection was made.

"I…I can see those colors," Rand murmured. "All around you."

Korden extended himself further, easing into the fusion of nebulous thoughts and shifting emotions that made up Rand Holcomb's psyche. There was some resistance at first, then the man relaxed and granted Korden admittance. From here, past all mental defenses, he understood that he could influence a person deeply, nudge their spectrums as he had with Meech in order to soothe his pain, but the very idea was too much like mind control for Korden's comfort. He held the bright point of Rand's focus and aimed it inward so they could search together for the eye of his conduit. The experience was like leading a person through dense trees made of a confusing array of color.

The passage was small and withered and tucked far back in Rand's dormant hindbrain. No wonder he didn't understand how he'd been accessing it. When they found it, Korden grabbed hold of the edges with his mind and strained against them, stretching the conduit wider.

The bridge came unsealed with a wet, puckered slurp, and a sputtering stream of artcraft spilled into the other man's consciousness.

Back in the real world, Rand flailed, slapping Korden's hands away from his temples. "What the fram was that?"

"The Upper," Korden told him. "The wellspring of His ever-burning love. It felt good, didn't it?"

"Y-yes," Rand panted. "It was like…a river of energy. Pure power coursing through me."

"I can try to show you how to use it. How to bend it to your will. And how to replenish it. If you want."

"Would that make you my…what was it? *Den-so*?"

"Technically. But you don't have to call me that if you don't want to."

"Good. Cause I don't." The other man thought for a long moment before saying, "No one can know. *Especially* not Lillam."

Korden tried not to betray his elation as he agreed.

Feeling Powerful

1

The thirst was relegated to an annoyance after they awoke and choked down the rank dasher milk, but it became a torment by the time they stopped for the day. They were all lightheaded, and none of them had needed to urinate since the day before, as their bodies put every iota of moisture in their systems to use. Korden's breathing was worse than ever in his life, every inhalation dragged kicking and screaming into his lungs, but his attempts to conjure potable water continued to meet with failure.

Dinner hydrated them a bit, enough to keep them steady. After eating, the four men trudged out to comb the Valley. Lillam wanted to help, but Rand made her stay to rest, with Zeega to watch over her.

Korden and Rand stuck close together and trekked in the opposite direction from Doaks and Meech. The desert night was moonless and near freezing, but they'd both brought coats. Once they got far from camp, a tense silence fell between them, until Rand broached the topic at hand.

"So...how does it work?" he asked, kneeling to hold a

waterskin beneath the dripping stem of a dasher. He sounded hoarse, as all of them did with their throats so parched. "I imagine something hard enough and it happens, right?"

Korden was using artcraft to wring every drop of moisture from another blossom a few pargs away, mangling the plant in the process. He could still sense that massive surplus of magic, but as long as he kept his emotions in check, he wasn't as worried about it growing beyond his control. "You have to learn to open the conduit on your own first."

"And what is that?"

"'The conduit is our sacred passage to the wellspring; faith is what maintains it,'" Korden recited. "It's what you experienced last night."

Keeping a watchful eye for scorpigators, Rand finished tapping the flower and moved to another along the side of the dune, spilling sand down the slope with every step. "All right then, I'm ready. Make me a believer. Tell me about this Upper."

"'The Upper unites all of humankind with His love. He oversees us and grants us strength and helps us to flourish in all our endeavors.'"

Rand froze with knife in hand and glanced over at him. "And?"

Korden frowned. "What do you mean?"

"That's it? 'He loves us and helps us?' Then how is he any different than the Aged Lord, or the Saint of Christ, or even Mother Tree?"

"Well, He's...the Great Interceder..."

"Does he have rules to live by? Are there sacred texts of

his teachings, like the Writ of Elderly Governance? Can you tell me stories of his deeds, like the Saint leading children away from the Filament with his magic flute?"

"No..."

The other man's aura showed bewilderment. "Then how am I supposed to have faith in the Upper if you can't tell me anything about him?"

Korden flushed with embarrassment and indignation. These were the same explanations Tash gave him so long ago, but they seemed childish when placed up against Rand's skepticism. "He grants us artcraft so that we can feel His presence. Does the Aged Lord do that?"

Rand put down the waterskin and knife and turned to face him. "All right, yes, I'll admit that what you showed me last night was incredible. It made me feel...powerful. But feeling powerful isn't something to believe in. If anything, it should be the other way around."

Korden rubbed his aching temples in frustration. How was he supposed to convey his creed to someone that didn't have his viewpoint? *Now you see how Zeega felt when you argued with her.* "Let's finish milking these and then we can try some faithing."

An hour and a half later, they sat cross-legged in the sand facing one another across a small, blue-flamed fire, eyes closed and concentrating. Rand followed Korden's instructions for this without question or protest, but came no closer to accessing the conduit for himself.

"I just can't find that place in my head you showed me."

"It took a lot of practice for me to keep my connection steady. Why don't we try crafting a *demno*? That's artificial light," Korden explained, before the other man could ask. He demonstrated this by making a small chunk of the hardpan glow, then handed another piece to Rand, who held it in his lap and stared at it.

"But I don't understand how light works," he said. "So how can I create it?"

"You're not understanding it, you're interpreting your personal concept of it. That's why mine is blue."

"The adjective, not the noun?"

"Exactly!"

Rand continued to hesitate. "But it needs to function in the real world, doesn't it? My eyes have to be able to see what it illuminates. What else is light, if not that?"

Korden shook his head while trying to remember if he'd ever asked Tash such questions. It all made so much more sense when he was young. The speech he'd given Zeega about asking questions floated through his thoughts. "You're overthinking it. Your imagination knows the properties of light even if your rational mind can't explain what creates them. Light is what fuels all our thoughts and dreams. It's the first thing we see when we're born. Without it, all we perceive is darkness. That's why this is one of the most basic elemental spells."

"Then…does that mean someone born blind couldn't do it?"

Korden sighed. "Just give it a try."

Rand shut his eyes. His *mohol* flared with concentration. Korden coached him, encouraging him to visualize the light, to see the rock glowing in his mind, but nothing happened.

"It's this thirst," Rand complained. "It's all I can think about."

"Could be a willpower problem," Korden agreed. "Or maybe your imagination is too weak. Have you ever played an instrument or drawn a picture? Artcraft usually flows best through those that have an artistic ability."

"Hildan always said I was a creative problem-solver." Rand grinned. "Could that be my art, keeping a settlement of fifteen-hundred people running smoothly?"

Korden gaped at him. "I...I don't know. Maybe."

"Some *den-so* you are. Seems like there's more you don't know about this whole business than what you do." Rand unfolded his legs and got up with a groan. "We better go back before the others get suspicious."

When they pooled their findings, they had enough dasher juice for all six of them to drink a full cup.

It did nothing to slake their thirst, and Stone's organ failure estimation lengthened by mere hours.

Korden fell asleep to the sound of his own breath wheezing in his ears.

2

"Sand spookies," Doaks proclaimed, nodding his head authoritatively. "I'm tellin yah."

"For the last time, there's no such thing as sand spookies, drude," Meech argued.

"Oh, then I suppose yah think the boy's 'Upper' brought this? Or maybe the lady's 'Aged Lord'? Or perhaps the Great Flyin Garbanzo Monster graced us with its presence in the middle of the night, eh?"

They stood in a circle around the discovery Korden had

made upon waking this morning. An arm's length from the wagon was a knee-high pedestal made of smooth, sculpted sand, as if it had grown out of the ground itself, like the monoliths and the walls of the crevies. Atop this pedestal sat a large basin also molded from the desert, and inside that basin, filled to the very brim, was what appeared to be sparklingly clear water, at least several gologas worth. The sight of it made Korden lick his cracked lips.

"You said it was sand spookies that toppled the spires over on us back in the canyon," Rand said, speaking without taking his eyes off the contents of the sand vessel.

"Prob'ly so, prob'ly so," Doaks agreed absentmindedly.

"Well, which is it? Do they want to kill us, or save us?"

Doaks seemed perturbed at the challenge to his authority on the subject. He opened his mouth to answer, but nothing came out. His brow wrinkled as he tried to reconcile the logic of his own claims.

"Is this what they're supposed to do?" Korden croaked, running a finger along the smooth rim of the basin. "Bring water?"

"I ain't never heard of this specifically, no," he admitted. "Or the spires, for that matter. But, like I said, it's all rumors. Mostly folks say they feel watched. Some others claim they saw the sand move on its own, like somethin took control of it."

"Sounds like whatever was helping me when I got sucked down," Lillam said softly.

"Ayuh, precisely, miss'um! That had to be them, too!"

Korden thought of that fleeting presence he'd sensed. He dipped a hand into the water. The liquid was surprisingly cool, untouched by the desert heat, although that surely wouldn't last long once the sun rose. He cupped a bit in his palm and lifted it to his mouth.

"Uh, Korden...you sure that's a good idea?" Rand lifted a hand as if to stop him and then let it flutter weakly back to his side. "Regardless of the sand spooky theory, we don't know where it came from."

"Someone obviously intended for us to drink it. And there's not much point in poisoning us when we're already dying. Might as well test it." He slurped the liquid up. It was heaven on his dry tongue. He wanted to gulp it down but forced himself to swish it around his mouth long enough for Stone to pronounce it safe.

That was all it took to convince the others. They drank greedily, like horses around a trough, no one calling to save any until they'd had their fill. The relief was instantaneous, a flood of strength into Korden's heavy limbs. His stomach sloshed pleasantly as he held Zeega's squishy body up so she could have her share as well, before Rand and Meech dunked a waterskin into the basin to drain the dregs. By that point, the pedestal was crumbling away in the wind as though it'd never existed.

"Three, maybe four days 'til we get to yah Prophet," Doaks said, as they climbed back aboard the wagon. "That is, if yah sure yah still wanna go."

"We're going," Korden insisted. "No matter what."

"Then I sure hope it's a smashin success, cause *that's* gonna be a hellsuva lot closer by then."

Korden looked to the west, where Doaks had pointed. A pall of dust rose into the air from somewhere on the horizon. It was much lighter than the maelstrom, the sort of cloud that could only have been made by hundreds of wheels churning up the desert sand.

Heater and his army were coming.

3

The next two days passed in much more pleasant manner. Every morning they were greeted with another basin of water, though they remained unable to catch their benefactors in the act. Since Zeega's roost atop the bonnet was destroyed, she began going deeper into the dunes at night to keep a watch for their visitors, while staying close enough for her call to prevent intrusions into Korden's sleeping mind. She claimed to have glimpsed the shifting aura once, but, other than that, the 'sand spookies'—for lack of a better term—slipped in and out of their midst without causing the slightest disturbance.

They travelled long hours during the days, conversing more than ever and playing totala, with even Lillam sitting in for a few hands. Something had changed among them, some unspoken easing of tension that was ironic, considering their worsening plight. That dust cloud was visible on the horizon each morning and dusk, when the wind was at its lowest, but without the Prophet's broadcasts, they had no way of telling how close the Incarnates were. As pledged, the voice on the radiowaves remained stubbornly silent. Stone, however, gave his own calculations, none of them encouraging.

And, each night, when their last meal was eaten and the rest of their group separated for sleep, Korden and Rand stole away from the camp and walked into the desert for artcraft lessons that continued to yield no results, both with and without focusing words.

"I just don't understand what I'm supposed to be thinking about," Rand told him, after another disastrous attempt at faithing.

"You're not supposed to be *thinking* about anything. You need to be able to clear your mind and feel the Upper, to know He's there, so that the artcraft can flow."

"Yes, but I *don't* feel him, and I *don't* know he's there, I already told you that!"

"But...but you *have* to!" Korden insisted, balling up his fists so tight the tendons in his fingers ached. He was at the end of his rope seeking ways to get the man to believe. Why couldn't faith be a thing that you just rolled up and forcibly shoved into someone's ear?

CONGRATULATIONS, SIR, Stone told him, the computer's tone wry. YOU HAVE DISCOVERED THE DRIVING MOTIVATOR FOR THE OVERWHELMING MAJORITY OF WARS FOUGHT BY HUMANKIND.

"I don't see why," Rand argued. He shook his head, then gave a knowing smirk as he tapped one temple. "Think about this: I didn't believe in him before when I stopped that bullet or did any of those other things. So why do I need to do it now?"

Korden took a moment to center himself, determined not to let frustration overtake him. Nevertheless, it was a valid question. Rand had told him about his fight with the scorpigator; a craftsman who could conjure at those levels should have no problem sensing *mohols* or lighting *demnos.* "Let's…take a break."

They uncurled from their faithing positions, and Korden stretched out on the sand. The grains were still warm, contrasting with the frigid night air. The sky above was clear and burned with a phalanx of stars, except for the dark hole in that corner which the Shroud occupied.

"Where did it come from?" Rand asked abruptly. "This magic? If your teachers taught you, then who taught them?"

"No one taught them. They awoke to it."

"*Awoke?*"

"Tash always said that artcraft is something we possessed a long time ago, but we forgot because we let ourselves become lazy and complacent with technology. When the Filament took all that away…we started to remember."

"Not me, apparently." Rand scooped up a handful of sand, letting it run through his fingers. Then he asked, with an unreserved hopefulness in his voice that Korden couldn't help but take as an insult, "Is it possible you were wrong? That I'm *not* a Crafter? Maybe there's some other explanation…"

"You did those things, Rand. You just can't do them on command." Korden sat up in alarm as a new thought came to him. "Strong emotion! That can affect your crafting, too! Maybe we need the right motivation! Think back to those times when you crafted. What were you feeling?"

Rand frowned as he retreated into memory. "Well, I was afraid I was going to die."

"That would be a hard condition to recreate."

"You sure?" Rand chuckled. "Cause it's happened a lot since I met you."

Korden sighed. "We'll keep trying. Something will work."

"Or maybe it's time I learn to play the lute." Rand was quiet for a bit, during which his *mohol* rippled with tones of worry and distress. Korden was about to ask if he was all right when he spoke again. "I know Lillam's wrong, that artcraft can't be passed like an infection, but...could your parents do it? Not this man Redfen, but your *real* parents. Do you even know?"

Korden lay back down so he didn't have to look at the other man. He knew the reason for the question—Rand's concern for his own child, still thinking of this ability as a shame rather than a gift—but this wasn't a topic he was prepared to discuss with anyone. Then again, perhaps honesty would be the best lesson he could impart as a *den-so*. "I was told that my mother was a Crafter. I never met her though, so I can't say for sure. She came into the town where Redfen lived, and they protected her while she gave birth. Then she gave me to him, and he ran."

"What about your father? What do you know of him?"

Korden took a deep breath before answering. "My mother told Redfen that I didn't have one."

He could feel Rand's gaze sharpen. "I don't understand."

"I don't either. She claimed that she'd never...with a man. That she just became pregnant."

Rand sat still, not speaking, the only noise the whispering shush of wind caressing the sand. Then he cleared his throat uncomfortably. "Korden, you're quite intelligent for your age. I would never claim otherwise. But this is one area where you might be a bit...inexperienced. So let me assure you...that is absolute and complete bullcurse."

Korden scowled, reminded of his conversation with Lillam about him being too young to understand the nature of love. "Why do you say that?"

"Because lots of women get themselves into that situation, and they're ashamed. Or they want to protect the name of their lover, the same way Lillam did for me. So they make up stories. That they were forced or tricked. Whatever they have to say to get others to take pity on them."

"My mother wouldn't do that!"

"How can you be sure, if you never met her?" Rand shook his head. "I mean, which is more likely? That a scared, pregnant woman told a whopping lie to gain the trust of people who could help her? Or that you're the third coming of the Saint of Christ?"

"I'm sorry I said anything," Korden huffed. "Let's keep practicing."

But the question stayed in the back of his mind for hours to come.

4

Just past noon on the third day after the maelstrom, Meech gave an eager shout. He stood on the back deck with the farviewers, looking to the northeast, and kept bawling, "I can see it! I can see the end of the Valley!" until Doaks stopped the wagon.

They all took turns peering through the double spyglass. Sure enough, far in the distance off to their right, a sparse green carpet of foliage replaced the orange sands of the desert, and it was no mirage this time. Seeing signs of life after so long in the sunbaked wasteland made something deep inside Korden yearn to run toward them.

"How soon till we get there?" Meech demanded. His *mohol* pulsed with an electric pink eagerness that entirely consumed him.

"Relax on, it's just an oasis," Doaks said. The swelling in his nose had gone down so much that his voice was returning to normal, but it would never sit straight on his face again.

"Shouldn't we try to get some water there?" Rand asked.

"Yes, let's do it!" Meech cried, bouncing on the balls of his feet.

Doaks's upper lip curled. "There's prob'ly enough below the surface for the plants to grow, but we'd have to dig to get it. Might be a waste of time, considerin our mysterious new friend is keepin us soggy."

"But who knows how long that will last?" Rand argued. "Isn't that why we're still heading toward the Prophet?"

"I'm followin orders on that account, rubo."

"We're so close now, we can't afford to stop," Korden said.

They left the oasis behind in their last hours of travel. That night, after another fruitless session with Rand, Korden plunged into sleep beneath the rear deck of the wagon.

And woke the next morning to a heavy rumble overhead as Gwenita rocketed away from him.

5

Rand's eyes flew open when he heard the familiar hum of the wagon's engine cycle up. He stood up so fast that the tent he shared with Lillam came loose from its support and collapsed on top of them. Rand wrestled free of the cloth in time to see the vehicle zooming away in the pale, pre-dawn light.

"*I told you!*" he howled, pulling on his tunic as he ran barefoot across the sand toward where Korden was sitting up. The cushion of light beneath the vehicle was the only visible part of their departing ride, a golden gleam speeding toward the reddish crack of the eastern horizon. "*I told you Doaks would stab us in the back the first chance he got!*"

"But...he promised..."

"And that shows you what his promises are worth!" Rand's anger was directed as much at himself; shouldn't he have expected such treachery after the man's proposal a few nights ago? "We never should've let that short little toad roam free!"

"Except the short little toad is right here."

Rand whirled. A few pargs away, Doaks was emerging from his own tent, with one hand on the small of his back. As they stared at him, Zeega came scuttling out of the dawn darkness to the west, her multiple eyes darting in different directions as she took in the situation.

That was everyone accounted for, but...

"Oh Meech," Rand groaned. He realized the wagon was heading back in the direction of the oasis. "You didn't."

Something crackled in the pile of blankets around Korden's bedroll. The boy lifted one corner to reveal the skins containing the last of their sand basin water, and one of the rectangular talkies. Meech's voice drifted from the device as Rand hurried toward it.

"Don't worry," his brother said. Even over the hissing connection, Rand could hear the shame in his voice. "I won't be gone long. I just...I'm sorry, drudes, but I'm not strong enough. I have to do this. I *need* it. Stay where you are, keep the talkie on, and I'll come back to get you, I promise."

Rand snatched up the box and pressed the button as he screamed, "*Meech, you framming cursehead, get back here right now! Do you hear me?*"

There was no reply. Doaks pointed at the red light on the side and said softly, "He either turned it off, or he's already outta range."

The strength drained out of Rand. He let the talkie fall and sank to his knees beside Korden. "It won't be some quick little jaunt like he says. If he finds some of that damn weed and starts pricking, he could be spun for *hours*."

Doaks held a hand up against the first shards of sunlight slicing over the horizon. "We'll all be good and roasted by then, rubos."

Behind him, Lillam began to sob.

"Zeega can catch him," a gurgly voice stated.

They all turned to the riftling.

"Are you sure?" Korden asked.

"Yes. The vehicle will outpace her, but Zeega will follow in its wake until the polluted human stops, then commandeer it. By whatever means necessary."

"What about the heat? You won't be riding on the wagon in the sun, you'll be *running* in it. Will you be able to take it?"

Several of her yellow eyes cast their gaze in different directions; on her alien face, Rand couldn't tell if it was an expression of nonchalance or hesitation. "Zeega does not know. But she sees little alternative."

"Then go." Korden pulled his necklace loose and tossed it to her, which she caught in a foreclaw. "Take Stone with you. He can tell you how to operate the wagon."

"And yah better bring this." Doaks tore off a thick swatch of fabric from his tent cloth, laid it on the sand, and backed away. She snatched the cloth up, then draped it over her small, lumpy body like a cape and cowl. "Take whatever yah want of the water, too. Yah'll prob'ly need it more'n us."

"Zeega will be unable to carry it and move quickly."

Rand cleared his throat. "If...if my brother won't come back with you...then leave him."

The riftling sought confirmation from Korden, who nodded hesitantly. Then she took off across the desert, moving so fast that her tentacles threw up a plume of warm sand in her wake.

OUTCAST

1

Meech's body was engulfed in searing flames, and the knowledge that they were only in his head did little to make them hurt less.

He thought he'd beaten his cravings. He really did. This period of forced sobriety in the desert had given him a mental clarity he hadn't experienced in years. But, as soon as he'd glimpsed that velvety green sea in the middle of the sand, the gimmies closed in around him like a steel trap, tightening and squeezing and smothering until his heart was on the verge of exploding inside his chest. He'd spent the night lying awake in his bedroll, sweating, shivering and warring with himself. As soon as it got light enough to see, he'd risen like a man in a dream, climbed aboard the wagon, and, after quietly leaving the talkie and waterskins beside Korden, he blasted off toward the oasis.

Even now, a sliver of remorse managed to surface through his aching need, like a glitter of mineral shining through the dirt in a prospector's pan. Aged Lord, what had he done? He couldn't leave them all back there in the middle of the desert, the sun would dry them out like jerky. Meech reached for the steering controls, meaning to spin the wagon around.

Drude, all they gotta do is sit in their tents, in the shade, and wait for you to come back. They'll barely even know you're gone.

But the Incarnates—

Are days away. Get to the oasis, grab all the jink you can get your hands on, and head back. It'll take you an hour, man. Two, tops.

Sounded like good advice to him. He pushed the lever that increased the vehicle's speed.

And yet, despite his interior voice's attempts to placate him, it took an hour and a half just to reach his destination, long after the sun began its blistering climb into the heavens. He was beginning to fear that he'd never find the oasis when he spotted that blip of green amid the orange sea.

Meech decreased his speed as he approached. The oasis couldn't be more than a span wide, growing in a roughly circular plot. The dominant vegetation appeared to be some variety of knee-high scrubgrass sprouting from the hardpan. A stunted, ugly plant tenacious enough to cling to life in the extreme heat of the Valley.

Exactly the sort of flora that jinkweed thrived amid. His heart soared.

But that wasn't all. Now that he was much closer, Meech could see the remains of rotting, old-world structures running in two neat rows through the center of the oasis, clustered on either side of what had once been a road. The water beneath this forgotten town and the plants feeding off it were surely the reason the dunes hadn't covered the place over long ago. The buildings reminded him of the ancient resort high above Tay-ho where he'd met Korden.

Thinking the boy's name caused another jab of shame. Some bodyguard he was turning out to be.

Meech stopped the wagon behind one of the sunbeaten structures, maneuvering it carefully through a collapsed wall and into the shade beneath the sagging roof. He leapt from the driver's seat and stumbled out into the scrubgrass, then fell to his knees and crawled, running his shaking hands through the foliage as he searched. What if this had all been for nothing, a wild ramlar chase? Sweat poured from his brow as the sun seared the back of his neck. Meech's bowels constricted from a sharp cramp that was caused more by panic than actual withdrawal.

C'mon, please, please be here, I NEED it...

The grasses seemed to part in front of him, laying down like subjects before their king, and there it was, the motherlode, a feathery sprout of the freshest jinkweed he'd ever seen in his life. He ripped it out in great fistfuls, shoving the plant, roots and all, into his dungaree pockets. A stash this big could last him weeks, well after they'd escaped the Valley.

Then why not take a taste now, drude? Sample the merchandise.

Meech's stomach clenched. No. No, he couldn't. He needed to get back to the others.

Yeah, but facing them ain't exactly gonna be pleasant. Imagine what they're gonna say. What Rand's *gonna say. Might as well be spun while you sit through the endless lectures.*

Again, he couldn't argue with the logic of that voice even though he knew—on some buried, semi-conscious level— it was the source of all his greatest misery in life. If he limited his dose, he would still be functional enough to get back.

Meech took one of the curled leaves from his pocket and ground it up in the palm of his hand. The juices flowed freely from this healthy plant, unlike the half-starved specimen he'd found that last morning in Tay-ho. His mouth watered at the sight; or would have, if it weren't so framming dry. He reopened one of the sores on his arms, having to scratch at the flesh with a ragged, bitten fingernail since it was mostly healed over.

Then he rubbed the raw sap into the bloody crater, forgetting the vow to limit his intake.

The narcotic entered his bloodstream, transforming his veins into threads of pure bliss. Meech lay back on the grass with a lazy grin, basking in the sun as the jinko took away his pain, his doubts, his fear. The sensation continued to grow, spreading throughout his body.

In fact, it was too much to bear now. A low moan escaped Meech's lips as all his senses burned with intolerable pleasure. He'd never experienced a spin like this before. He wondered briefly if it could be because he hadn't pricked in so long, but then recalled something Jaimer once told him, about how jinkweed strains become less robust the more they're harvested. Meech could envision his old spinning buddy sitting beside a guttering fire, eyes glazed over, as he drawled, "Mosta the jinks 'round Tay-ho have, um, like, less'n a tenth of their natural potency, man. And the pure stuff? Drude...that curse would gut-punch even me, but a lightweight like you? Heh, good luck."

If that were true and not just spun talk, then could this patch of jinko growing out here in the middle of the Valley, untouched by human hands, be so strong that it *harmed* him?

As if to answer this question, another wave of ecstasy caused him to cry out. This wasn't enjoyable. Not in the least. The euphoria was cruel in its intensity, changing him, stretching his brain like warm taffy, melting the skin off his bones. He reached to the place on his forearm where he'd injected the jinko and clawed at the flesh in a futile attempt to drain the drug back out of his system, ripped and tore until blood flowed freely down his hand and pattered onto the ground, where the greedy sand sucked up the moisture immediately. Then Meech's muscles began to twitch and flex so much, he was reduced to a shivering ball on the desert floor.

"This is exactly why I didn't want to bring you with me," a voice said, cutting through his misery.

Meech's neck felt brittle and yet slack and boneless at the same time, but he somehow forced his head to turn so he could look up at the speaker. Though his vision wavered, he could identify the person standing over him. "K-Korden? How d-did you—"

The boy that he'd come to worship as a hero crossed his arms and shook his head sadly. "I knew it. I knew you couldn't be trusted from the minute I laid eyes on you. That's why I left you behind when I went to get the batteries, because I knew you'd find a way to fram it all up. You're even worse than Doaks; at least *he* serves a purpose, but you're just dead weight."

"N-no," Meech croaked. "You d-don't understand…"

"What's to understand?" Rand materialized beside Korden out of thin air. His mouth was set in a firm line, that familiar look of disappointment in his eyes as he stared down at Meech. "I've said the same thing about you for years, little brother. You're hopeless. Beyond redemption. I was going to let Hildan kick you out of Ida without so much as a word in your defense. And I sure wouldn't be here with you now if I didn't need Korden's help. When you think about it, I've been trying to get rid of you since we were kids, but you never take the hint."

"Please don't s-say that. I can change…this isn't m-me, I'm not b-bad…"

"Oh really?" His brother laughed. "If this isn't you, Meech, then who the hells is? I've certainly never met him. But if you won't believe me, maybe you'll listen to *them*."

Meech sensed a new presence to his right. He jerked his face around to find two people standing in the scrubgrass, a man and a woman holding hands. Though their faces were blurred and indistinguishable, he recognized them from their shabby, stained clothes, the last thing he'd seen them wearing when he was seven years old.

"Mom?" Meech rasped. "D-Dad?"

"We left because of you," his father said simply, giving voice to the secret fear that had plagued Meech most of his life. "We were perfectly content going on a Rearing for Rand's sake. But once you came along, and got old enough for us to see what you were like…"

"That's right," his mother agreed, the words issuing from the smear of color that served as her face, a face whose details Meech had never been able to recall no matter how hard he tried. "I was ashamed that my womb could conceive a creature as lowly as you. You were an embarrassment that we would've done anything to be rid of."

"Not true," Meech sobbed. Tears streamed down his cheeks, as caustic as acid. "You're l-lying, that's not t-true…"

They all began to laugh then, harsh, mocking peals that echoed inside his skull. He crawled backward across the blazing sand as all four of them advanced on him, their laughter becoming inhuman growls, then curled into a ball and covered his ears.

Finally…mercifully…unconsciousness took him.

2

He had no idea how long he lay there, caught between life and death, before an odd rasping sound brought him swimming up from the depths of delirium. His skin was pink with sunburn and screamed when he moved. Meech sat up, head aching but much clearer. The ruthless laughter of his parents and Rand and Korden was fresh in his mind, but at least now he saw that they were only hallucinations now.

Meech cocked an ear toward the noise, a protracted scraping that was just audible over the sigh of the desert wind. It seemed to be coming up the middle of the road from the south, growing louder as it neared. No way could he stand up, so he got back to his hands and knees and crawled into the closest building—a ramshackle structure that was little more than a wooden frame—until he reached an empty window at the front. Lying beneath it, he poked his head up to see onto the street…

…and gawked at what was out there.

Several men that lived high in the snowy mountains around Ida travelled by dog sled, so Meech was well aware of what such conveyances looked like. And that's what he was seeing now: a tiny sleigh with modified skids for slicing through the sand, rather than the broad runners meant to skim across snow. And, instead of canines, a team of creatures like Zeega was hooked up to the front, pulling the sled along. They varied in size—although all of them were far larger than Korden's companion—and they appeared to be having difficulty with their task, huffing and wheezing and a few even quivering as their purple appendages sank deep into the sand with each labored step. Of the driver, nothing was visible; he or she was hidden by a wooden shack that completely enclosed the pilot's seat of the sled.

Meech rose up from his hiding spot, meaning to call out to them, perhaps tell them that he knew one of their relatives, when a tentacle slid over his mouth and sudden weight forced his head back down. Five yellow eyes gazed into his.

"Do not make a sound if you wish to live, human," Zeega whispered.

3

Riftlings might be more resilient than humans, but Zeega suspected if she'd attempted the trip across the desert any later in the day, during the worst of the heat, it would've been the end of her. Her small body was on the verge of total shutdown by the time she scurried into the fringes of the oasis, a fact that Stone—now dangling from the indentation where her head joined her body—was more than happy to remind her of. The moment she entered the grasses, Zeega dug a furious hole in the sand to reach the moisture level, then slurped urgently at the dampness she found there.

Once replenished, she shifted her attention back to the hunt. She'd quickly lost sight of the wagon, but she could follow the human's mental scent for spans upon spans, if necessary. Zeega sensed him somewhere ahead, in one of the abandoned dwellings.

WARNING! SENSORY SCANS DETECT APPROACHING LIFE FORMS!

Zeega is aware, she snapped at the computer. *Zeega is not some feeble human that cannot utilize its own perception organs effectively!*

MY APOLOGIES, MY INTENT WAS TO—

Be silent and let Zeega think.

She could sense the black aura of an Incarnate, but discerned a brood of fellow *hoshnitaths* only from their physical sounds and smells. After stopping the foolish human named Meech from revealing himself, she emitted her call, attuning the mental blocker to stifle his thoughtwaves. Then she took his place at the window and observed the approaching sand skiff. No doubt this group was coming for Korden, heeding the call for the Filament's soldiers far and wide to converge upon this desert.

The brood pulling the conveyance was in visible distress,

overheated and overworked. As they reached the center of the oasis, several riftlings stumbled and collapsed on the sunbaked crete where a road had once been, bringing the whole party to a stop.

The rickety wooden door of the skiff cockpit crashed open. A burly male *Exatraedes*—dressed in a form-fitting black outfit that covered the entire body, overlaid by various pieces of rusted battle armor and a thick chainmail cowl that kept his heavily scarred face out of the sun—leapt onto the ground.

As soon as she saw him, an impulse rose in Zeega: the urge to kneel before him, to surrender herself to whatever punishments the masters saw fit, if it meant a chance of getting back in their good graces. But she stamped out this instinct like the embers of a fire before the blaze could spread and overwhelm her.

The Incarnate barged down the line of riftlings, administering vicious kicks to those who'd fallen. "*Get up!*" he roared. "*Keep moving! I didn't call a stop!*"

The largest of the riftlings, undoubtedly the broodminder, uncoupled from its position at the head of the entourage and approached the demon with head lowered submissively.

"Massssster," it began, speaking with the hissing impediment that the most cowed *hoshnitaths* tended to get with human language. "The brood issss exhausssssted, many clossse to death. Pothi begsss you to grant a brief ressst ssso they may be revived."

The Incarnate scrabbled beneath his chest armor and yanked a coiled whip free from its belt. The lash made of braided leather, the end shredded and tipped with glittering shards of glass. He wielded it expertly, flicking it high into the air and then bringing it cracking down across the back of the broodminder.

With its head down, the riftling never saw the blow coming. It screeched and backpedaled, jellied flesh torn in several places so that viscous, violet-sheened blood dripped down its side.

Zeega had seen such treatment of her species at the hands of the *Exatraedes* every day of her life.

But never had the sight filled her with such rage.

"There will be no rest!" the Incarnate growled. "The boy is close, you all must sense it just as I do! We will take him ourselves and have him trussed and waiting when Regent Torgas's new ally arrives! Is that clear?"

"Yesss, Massster!" Pothi, the broodminder, groveled. The others added their agreements. Those on the ground climbed wearily to their *versicrods*...except for the smallest member, which flopped right back over. The Incarnate rushed to it and brought the whip whistling down.

"*GET UP!*" he bellowed. The riftling tried again, shaking with the strain, but couldn't comply. The Incarnate raged, hitting it with the whip over and over. "*STAND OR I!*" *CRACK!* "*WILL FLAY YOU!*" *CRACK!* "*TIL THERE'S NOTHING LEFT!*" *CRACK!*

MUSCLE TENSION REVEALS WHAT YOU ARE CONTEMPLATING, Stone said, AND I MUST URGE YOU TO—

Zeega bolted through the empty windowframe, leaving Meech on the ground.

She barreled into the back of the Incarnate's legs, causing him to stumble before the whip could crack. He spun, red eyes flashing, fury on his face, but she scaled his armor before he could make a move. Her tentacles gripped his shoulders while her good foreclaw slipped through the chainmail collar and sank into the vulnerable skin of his throat, ripping a hole in the flesh. Zeega leapt away as he sank to his knees, clutching the wound. The Incarnate attempted to staunch the tide of brackish gore, then crashed over onto his side and lay unmoving while the *animoga* squirted from his eyes, seeking another host. After a few moments, the miniature stormcloud dissipated, and his body began to putrefy in the sun.

4

The collective gaze of the brood fell upon Zeega, who stood ramrod straight, tension turning every tentacle as rigid as wood. Their dark faces and yellow eyes conveyed shock…but that changed as soon as Pothi stepped forward and yipped in the gargled *hoshnitath* tongue, "It is the apostate! The traitor! The one the masters warned of!"

This was nothing less than what she expected, but the accusation still stung. She stood her ground as more of the brood unhooked from the skiff and advanced on her, baring their daggerlike teeth.

"This one rejects the Filament, rejects the Stranger!" Pothi declared. The broodminder was far larger than her, would have no trouble extinguishing her *yan* singularly, let alone with the rest of the brood. "It serves the boy now! Pothi's brood must—"

"You are free," Zeega told them.

Confusion flickered across Pothi's features. "What…did you say?"

"The masters have deceived the *hoshnitaths*. They are... liars. You do not have to obey them any longer."

Silence. The other members of the brood looked uncertainly to Pothi, who was observing Zeega with a curious mixture of disgust and fear. After a moment, the broodminder relented and backed away from her, then said to the others, "Put those unable to run aboard the skiff, then prepare to leave. Pothi's brood will return to the masters for new orders."

Something inside Zeega sank. She didn't know what she'd hoped to achieve by conveying to them the same ideas which had infected her own mind, but at least they seemed too frightened of her now to attack. She watched as the infirm members were helped to the pilot's seat. The riftling who'd been beaten had to be lifted by several of its broodmates. Its body was a torn, bleeding mess...but Zeega could swear that it looked at her with gratitude when it was carried past.

Pothi scowled as the brood took their places at the skiff's yoke. "You are outcast. Dead to all *hoshnitaths*. And you will pay for your sins." The words were strident and determined...but that fear remained in all eleven of the broodminder's eyes as the threat was declared.

Zeega watched the skiff slide off across the desert, then hurried back toward Meech.

EMOTIONAL SPEECH

1

Meech and Zeega had been gone little more than an hour, and already the heat was excruciating.

Korden strung the tents together to make one large shelter for the four of them. They sat huddled in the scant shade beneath, not moving or speaking to conserve energy, while they waited for the talkie to give word of their salvation. Except for Rand, that is; he muttered under his breath about his brother while fanning Lillam, who appeared more tired and sickly than ever before. Her aura had taken on a dark green tinge at its core that Korden didn't like.

Doaks—stripped out of his fine suit down to breeches and a breezy cotton tunic—wiped a thick sheen of sweat from his forehead and held up the waterskin. "We should drink this now, 'fore the heat gets to it."

Korden frowned. "Shouldn't we save it? What if…?"

"What if *nothing*. The octopus is either gonna come back or she ain't. Holdin on to this 'til we die of heatstroke ain't gonna do anybody any good."

"Don't say that," Rand chided sharply.

Doaks cocked one bushy eyebrow at him. "Deludin ourselves ain't gonna help much neither, rubo."

Lillam delivered a throaty, hacking cough. Rand snatched the waterskin and offered it to her. She took a swallow, then asked in a strained, thin voice, "Are we close enough to the Prophet that we could walk if we had to?"

"With Gwenita, I figgered we'd get there sometime early tomorrow. On foot though…we'd never make it. Hells, I don't even think we'll survive like this but another couple hours."

The estimate was alarming, but Korden barely heard it. His attention had been drawn beyond the tent, where he caught a glimpse of flickering color moving through the sand. He crawled outside and stood scanning the dunes, the direct sunlight a burning brand against his bare flesh.

"What is it?" Rand asked. The faces of the others gathered in the tent opening, staring out at him.

"*Hey!*" Korden cupped his hands around his mouth and shouted into the vast emptiness of the Valley. "*If you're out there, we need help!*" He thought of the stranded caravan as he made this similar plea and winced at the accompanying guilt. Now he understood their desperation, although he didn't think it would ever drive him to the lengths that Knox and his men were willing to go to.

The heat scorched his words to cinders as they came out of his mouth. For an interminably long time, the only response was the dry scrape of the wind. Korden had just about given up when the ground in front of him started to quake. He leapt away, fearing more suck sand, but the desert floor was shifting rather than sinking, separating and tearing apart to reveal a dark cleft. It continued to widen until the motion stopped as suddenly as it began.

A neat, round hole sat a few pargs away from him, with a ramp made of sand descending into the depths of the earth.

2

"We can't go down there," Rand argued, as they stared into the pit. The walls of the sand tunnel—which reminded him of the unnaturally smooth sides of the crevies—quickly faded into darkness beyond the opening, offering no hint at what might lie in wait.

"Why?" Korden asked. The kid looked genuinely confused, much to Rand's frustration.

"Because it could be a trap to bury us alive. Like the spires dropping on us in that canyon."

"But...the sand spookies gave us the water."

"*Did* they? We have no way to be sure that whoever has been giving us the water is the same one that created this hole in the ground. Or even why they gave it to us in the first place. Maybe they kept us alive just long enough to get us here."

Korden made a show of glancing at the landscape around them. "I can't see that here is any different than the rest of the Valley."

"You know what I mean, damn it."

"Yes, I know what you mean, Rand. What I don't know," he gave Rand a pointed look, "is why you can't seem to have faith. In anything at all."

Rand stared daggers back at him, daring the boy to say more. "Because faith is just trust that hasn't been earned."

"Well, yah rubos can debate all yah want," Doaks said, clipping the talkie onto his belt. "As for me, I'm goin in, since there ain't much else to do up here but die."

He stepped onto the ramp—but did so gingerly, Rand noted, as though testing its give—then ducked his head beneath the opening and descended. Korden followed close behind.

Rand looked to Lillam. She shrugged, the gesture itself appearing to tax her, and said, "The sand spookies…or whatever they are…they helped me, Rand. I *do* trust them." She stepped down the ramp and, after the smallest delay, he did the same.

The tunnel was wide enough for them to walk single file, the ceiling so low it forced them to hunch. The gentle slope continued, but they were soon walking in darkness. Rand saw Korden dig a large rock from the smooth wall and imbue it with that glowing blue light.

Lillam drew away from the show of magic with a small, guttural sound of disgust, pressing back against him. Which led Rand to the question he'd been asking himself ever since his lessons began: if he came to master Korden's mystical arts, did he intend to hide it from Lillam for the rest of their lives?

At the front of the procession, Doaks mumbled, "Gettin cooler."

Now that he mentioned it, Rand could feel the desert heat dropping away, replaced by a blessed briskness that chilled the sweat on his face. He looked back and saw that the entrance was a distant yellow coin high above their heads.

A few more paces, and the incline evened out. They stepped into a much larger underground chamber, where the walls and roof were all made of rounded sand, without any straight edges. There were no other passages or exits, just this empty bubble in the earth, but the higher ceiling allowed them to stand up straight. The blue glow coming from the rock in Korden's palm reflected off tiny chips of mineral around them, creating a strange, sparkling illumination, like a Stilling night sky full of cold stars.

"How deep do you think we are?" Korden's breath plumed in the frigid air as he spoke.

"Deep," Doaks confirmed. The squat man stood on his toes to brush his fingertips on the top of the chamber, causing sand to loosen and rain down. "Far enough that the heat from the sun never makes it down here."

Lillam rubbed at her bare arms, where gooseflesh had broken out. The circles under her eyes looked even darker in the shadows. "What do we do now?"

"We wait. Be a lot easier to survive in this temperature than up in the heat."

Rand shook his head urgently. "But what if—?"

Doaks cut him off with a groan. "Would yah shut yah gob and enjoy the bright side for once? Aged be, I've heard of lookin gift horses in the mouth, but yah really stick yah whole head in, don't yah?"

Lillam gave a tired chuckle as she leaned against the wall and closed her eyes.

Rand fought the urge to shove the 'bright side' right down the man's throat. Fuming, he turned back to the exit from this underground cavern, intending to stomp right back out, but let out a squawk when he saw the silhouette blocking his path.

3

Korden moved protectively in front of the others as they faced the figure that had appeared in their midst. Rand had been right, he thought, to not want them coming down here. This pleasantly cool chamber made him feel as trapped as Loathe's cave with the newcomer standing in front of the sole exit. He held up his *demno* to shed more light on the intruder and gaped in confusion at what was revealed.

The figure was shaped like a person, but sculpted from smooth, featureless sand. Its head was nothing but a blank oblong, no features whatsoever, and the appendages that served as its arms had no fingers or even discernible hands, just blunt, rounded ends. It reminded him of the wooden doll Port used for his sketches back in the village, a fully poseable statuette meant to mimic the human form, but even that model held more detail than this rudimentary sand creature. As they stared, it raised one of its blunt limbs; not in greeting, it seemed, but with a sense of wonder, as though figuring out how to move it.

Then Korden opened the conduit's eye and saw the truth.

The figure had an aura. Not around it, but *inside* it, buried within the sand. The spectrum shifted through an array of subtle colors faster than Korden could interpret them, but he recognized it all the same.

"You gave us the water," he ventured, not sure if the entity could even understand him. "You're the thing that's been following us."

Yes. Hope form this did not you startle. Familiar more to

you I believed would it be.

Behind Korden, Lillam gasped in surprise, mirroring his own shock.

Because the strange jumble of words hadn't been received through their ears or even broadcast into their heads, as with Stone's telepathic communications. It had been, well...*felt* was the only way Korden could describe it. A rush of complex emotions that somehow conveyed a message which their minds could interpret as language. He glanced back and saw that all three of his companions' *mohols* were lit up with the same shimmering display as the newcomer, as if they'd been infected.

"It's like the feelings you get from a beautiful song, or a familiar smell," Lillam summed up softly, as the borrowed emotions faded. "They tell a story. Well...one where the words are all mixed up."

Korden nodded at the comparison. The experience was surreal, but not at all unpleasant.

The aura inside the sandman pulsed, and the dynamic shift of colors slowed drastically. Sorry am I, if hard to understand. Emotion less is structured than speech your. Condense into words difficult, but will try.

"Hot damn," Doaks whispered. He rubbed the palm of one hand on his barrel chest as through trying to massage his heart. "A real-life sand spookie."

"You're...made of pure emotion," Korden surmised.

Yes. People my are called—there was a blank place here in the communication, where a complicated twinge of emotion made Korden shiver—Beings of form no physical, only feeling.

"My name is Korden. This is Rand, Lillam, and Tarmon."

A pleasurable rush washed through Korden that he took to be delight at making their acquaintance. The being didn't offer its own name, but Korden figured it would probably be as untranslatable as its species. If it had a name at all, that is.

From the corner of his eye, he saw Doaks make a broad, sweeping gesture to encompass the subterranean chamber and the sandman itself. "Yah may not be tangible, but yah don't seem to have a problem controllin things that are."

Particles tiny only. Bent easily to will our. So, mastery complete over sand have we.

"That is incredible, my friend. Listen, I have a little stage show I think yah'd be perfect for—"

"You stopped me from falling in the suck sand," Lillam interrupted. Her pale face was solemn as she added, "Thank you for that."

Welcome are you.

"But what do you *want*?" Rand asked, not bothering to hide the suspicion in his voice. Beside him, Lillam grimaced uncomfortably. "Why are you helping us?"

The blank face of the sandman shifted. A curved line appeared near the bottom that Korden recognized as a smile. One of the blunt arms swung clumsily in his direction. When it 'spoke' again, the message was emphasized with passion. Because sense us this one could! Has not with humans that happened!

"It's called artcraft." Korden grinned back. "I can see you as colors inside the sand. Like a rainbow."

Do not know about 'rainbow', but fascinating is perception

your. Could not let you die no matter what declared my—another one of those broken places in the communication, but this time Korden thought he got the gist of the emotional mixture.

"Your...family? Parents? They didn't want you to help us?"

No. Forbade they communication with lifeforms all. Existence our remain must a secret. Made canyons this land across, travelers to discourage.

Doaks gasped. "The crevies! Yah responsible for the crevies!"

Yes. Constantly change to confusion create. But humans stubborn so, continued to come desert into.

"Ayuh, that's us. Stubborn humans. I suppose it was yah that made the spires out around the mesas, too."

Religious are they. Of home the piece only allowed ourselves.

"Then why did you knock them over on top of us?" Rand demanded.

The grin on the sandman's face fell. His next words were filled with chagrin. Overzealous can my 'family' be. Us sense could you, so departure your hasten they attempt. Terrified they are of discovery on plane this.

"Wait on...you're not from this plane?" Korden latched onto the phrase, thinking of his talk with the Incarnate that possessed Allin back in the village. Doaks hissed in his ear, "*What's a plane?*" but Korden ignored him as he asked, "Where did you come from?"

The sandman considered this. Korden couldn't figure out if it was deciding whether to tell its story, or *how* to tell it. Homeworld on our, sand is all. Great structures, society of millions. Emotional state allowed us behind to leave war and killing, Paradise was it. The *mohol* shifted through a sorrowful band of colors. Gone all, now.

"How?" Lillam sounded deeply concerned even as she paused to cough into one fist. "What happened?"

The thing same happening world to your. And then the sandman exuded one word tinged with so much hate that the emotion caused pain to flash through Korden's skull:

FILAMENT.

It needed no prompting to continue. Swept they through world our without warning. No weapons we had, nor will to fight. Stole they hope, destroyed homes, and smothered world our in darkness.

Korden found tears rolling down his cheeks at the utter loss and devastation woven into the sandman's message; he wiped them away before the air in the underground chamber could chill them on his skin. He was literally able to *share* this being's pain through its words, the ultimate form of empathy.

"Then how'd yah get here?" Doaks asked, and Korden was surprised to hear weepy roughness in his voice.

Planes many are there in the allverse. *Allverse*: another term that rang bells for Korden; he had to think hard to recall that it was Loathe who'd previously used the word. The Filament in them rips holes to continue plunder their. Used one my family to escape, centuries ago countless. Realities many moved through before settling yours in, recreating home here.

"You're refugees." Korden thought of the many stories Stone told him of people fleeing the Dark Filament's advance right here on their own planet, whole nations evacuating before the Shroud covered them. He'd seen evidence of this with his own eyes: dead autos piled up on an ancient roadway like the metal backbone of some great serpent.

Yes. Such exiles across the allverse stream, sanctuary seeking in planes which the Filament has breached. Attempt some to warn their homes new, to a rebellion prepare. Others, us like, live want only.

"And some use the opportunity for their own gain," Korden added, as Loathe's voice whispered in his ear, *We have dined on the most inventive minds the allverse has to offer.*

So much very, the sandman confirmed sadly. Not just beings sentient. Lifematter and creatures foreign contaminate ecologies. Interbreed, evolve. Reshape worlds entire.

"The Great Species Emergence," Korden said, using the term that the last scientists of the Purge had coined hundreds of years ago for all the strange new animals and plants popping up rapidly across the face of the planet.

Now he recalled a day several years before, when smoke had been visible on the horizon north of the village, and a flood of animals streamed out of the forest. Deer and chipmunks and elk and snakes and even a few maldin stampeded through their home, consumed by terrified auras. Redfen told him they were fleeing a fire, and the Olders kept a watch for days to see if the flames would shift in their direction.

That's exactly what the Dark Filament is, he thought. *A forest fire that everyone flees from.*

Rand spoke up once more, that naked suspicion mostly—but not completely—gone. "How many of you are there?

How many escaped your home?"

Eight. More perhaps refuge sought in planes other, but know we don't.

"And you've been out here haunting the desert this whole time? You didn't even *try* to help us?"

"Rand…" Lillam placed a restraining hand on his arm.

The sandman's aura bristled as a crooked frown etched itself onto the blank face. When arrived, invasion under way was well. Collapsed had society your already. Nothing could do we.

Rand stepped past Korden and jabbed a finger into its chest, spilling a shower of granules. His anger seemed to be drowning out the effect of the being's presence in his aura. "You could've revealed yourself to those that were left! Shared what you knew about this…this *allverse*! Helped us leave the same way you did!"

Last of kind our, are we. The message was delivered amid a complicated burst of shame and reproach. If to Filament revealed, us hunt would they. Species our preserved must be. When world this begins decline final, a tear to plane new will we seek.

Rand threw a hand up and walked away to the back of the cavern, spraying a cold fog of breath over his shoulder as he snapped, "Oh yes, keep running and save yourselves, right?"

Doaks snorted. "Don't get so high and mighty there, rubo. Yah stood front and center with those gents we left to fend for themselves."

"That was different!"

"Oh, ayuh, I'm sure it was. For *yah*."

"One more word from you, Doaks, and I swear…"

The sandman turned back to Korden, resting its crude arms on his shoulders. *The army Filament this way coming. After you are they?*

"Yes."

Sorry am I. Ride they now day and night in eagerness. Delay with canyons I tried, but upon you will they be in hours. More nothing can do I to help, or discovered people my could be.

"That's all right." Korden tried to exude positivity, in case this being was reading their emotions in kind. "You should get far away from us, so they don't find you."

The sandman nodded sadly. *Chamber this will remain for as long as needed.*

"Actually, there's one other thing you could do," Korden told the being. "Another group of humans was stranded to the west. If they're...still alive...will you give them water, like you did for us? Help them to get out of the desert? We promised to send help."

It will done be. With that, the being gave him a pat, sent a rush of emotions through him that Korden interpreted as 'Good luck,' and the figure collapsed into a shower of loose soil. Korden saw the *mohol* flit through the wall of the underground chamber, disappearing amid the desert sands.

4

"'Allverse?'" Both of Doaks's bushy eyebrows climbed high up his brow. "'Planes?' What the hells was that thing talkin about, kid? What're yah involved in?"

"I don't know," Korden told him truthfully. He felt like he'd been given several pieces to a puzzle, but whatever picture they formed was too vast for him to comprehend their placement in it. "But I think we learned more about the Dark Filament than anyone in history." He frowned thoughtfully. "Well, *our* history, anyway."

"Oh, that's wonderful! Fat lot of good that'll do us when they're tearing us apart in a few hours!" Rand stood at the rear of the chamber with his back to them. He held his head in both hands and groaned, "Aged Lord, this was a mistake. This was *all* a mistake."

"How much is 'all'?" Lillam asked quietly.

Rand looked at her, but said nothing.

"Go ahead, say on," she urged. She trembled all over, her aura returning to that sickly greenish tint. "You haven't wanted this baby from the start."

"*Of course I didn't!*" he shouted, the words oddly muffled in the chamber. "*I never made any secret of that, did I?*"

"No. But you *did* make a choice to leave everything behind and come with me. And since then, you've taken out your anger and frustration on everyone else."

"*That's completely unfair! Hells, for all I know, you planned this all along!*"

Lillam's eyes bulged from their sockets. "*What?*"

Doubt flashed across Rand's face, but he'd come too far to back down now. "*That's right! Maybe you secretly wanted a child, but needed some poor dupe to help you take care of it! The highest man in town looked like the best bet, didn't he?*"

"*You weren't 'the highest man in town,' Rand Holcomb!*" she shrieked. "*But I sure wish I HAD gotten banged up by Hildan; he wouldn't have whined and puled as much as you!"*

"Don't fight," Korden admonished. "We have much bigger problems right now."

"We sure do." Doaks's dark eyes studied Korden. From the silver flashes in his *mohol*, he knew what the salesman was going to say next. "Kid…it might be time to face the music. It's *yah* those Incarnates want. Yah leave now, get some distance from us…they might not even find us." He bit the inside of his cheek and added, in the most nonchalant of tones, "That is…if yah wanna save the life of yonder unborn rubo."

Lillam took a shambling step toward him, one hand laid protectively over her stomach. Her voice was high with anger as she told him, "You said yourself he's too young to be putting all our expectations on him!"

Doaks glowered. "I'm not puttin anything on him except cold, hard truth. What he does with it is up to him."

A deep chill penetrated all the way to Korden's bones, but it had nothing to do with the cool air. He looked to Rand, but the man stared at the ground. His aura, however, told Korden everything he needed to know about where he stood in this debate.

"I'll do it," Korden said. "I'll go."

At the same moment, Lillam collapsed to the floor with a horrible *thud.*

5

Rand saw her swoon, but he was too far away to catch her. Lillam wilted like a dying flower, hunching and shriveling as she sank to her knees and then pitched over backward on the cold sand. He knelt at her side and saw through her fluttering eyelids that her eyes were rolled back in her head.

"Lillam?" He patted her cheeks; they were warm with fever even in the frigid chamber. "Lillam, sweetlove, wake up! Can you hear me? What's wrong?" The only response was a high, piteous moan from deep in her throat. Rand jerked his head around and found Korden. "What did that thing do to her?"

Before the boy could answer, Doaks pointed. "Her shoulder."

Rand looked at the tunic she wore. It was one of his, so the neck hole was far too large, revealing a dark discoloration creeping across her delicate collarbone. He grabbed hold of the garment and tore it open, revealing the shooter wound in her upper arm that she'd received on their flight out of Ida. The edges appeared raw, and pus oozed through the clumsy stitches he'd given her. In the blue glow from Korden's rock, the veins leading away from the wound took on a horrible livid purple color beneath her skin.

"That's living rot," Doaks said. "Yah didn't see the wound was that bad?"

"She...she told me it was better," Rand insisted. "With everything that's happened, I...I didn't have time to worry about it." *Which is precisely why she lied.*

"Yah'd need some powerful medicine to fight off rot that advanced. Course, if all my belongins hadn't been burned, maybe I could've cobbled somethin to get her by..."

A terrible panic seized Rand. This couldn't be happening,

not after what he'd just said to her. In his guiltridden mind, those cruel words might as well have caused this, and now he would never be able to take them back. He tore his gaze away from the blight that was consuming the woman he loved and fixed it on Korden, whose eyes he couldn't bear to meet a minute before.

"Please," he pleaded. "Can you do anything to help her?"

6

Lillam's *mohol* was overrun with that foul green murk. Korden approached tentatively, her earlier rebukes fresh in his memory. He expected her to scream at him when he knelt opposite Rand and laid his hands gently on either side of the injury.

Korden closed his physical eyes and sent the one inside the conduit questing out, exploring the infected wound the same as when he'd healed his broken hand.

Dull red squiggles leapt out of the darkness at him, a delicate tracery of tainted veins. They gave sickly pulses of heat in tune with Lillam's heartbeat as the poison coursed through them, working deeper into her body, decaying the flesh and clogging the bloodways with rot.

A malady this bad was nothing like fractured bones. He could do serious harm to her if the healing went awry.

She's going to die anyway if you do nothing.

Finding no reasonable rebuttal to that logic, Korden concentrated.

He needed a delicate approach and a tight grip on the

conduit to keep the flow of artcraft from slipping beyond his control. His knowledge of anatomy was limited, his understanding of diseases elementary, so he imagined myriad tiny nets in her bloodstream, filtering out the infection and forcing it back toward the wound entry. He envisioned razors carefully carving away the dead tissue so that it, too, could be drawn out. It was a mechanical approach to a chemical problem, but it was all he could think to do.

Doaks, hovering over his shoulder, gave a low, appreciative whistle.

Korden opened his eyes. The darkness in Lillam's veins was slowly shrinking, receding back toward the source. He refocused and willed harder, increasing the flow of artcraft in increments, visualizing until the conduit throbbed in the center of his mind like a migraine. Seconds ticked by. Then he felt a gush of warmth across his hands and looked down to see putrid, yellow-green fluid spurting from the hole in her shoulder.

Lillam's eyes opened. Bewilderment etched her feverish brow. She registered Rand, then Korden, and her confusion was replaced by abject terror. He thought she was about to yell at him, but she cried, "The baby, is she…? Please tell me she's all right!"

Korden took one of her hands. She struggled for a moment before submitting. He held his other out to Rand, who accepted it with a questioning frown and then, at Korden's nod, picked up Lillam's other hand, forming a circle between the three of them as the Moambati sisters did in his dream.

Korden reached for their auras, connecting their minds

to his own. He was working purely on instinct now, feeling his way through artcrafts he only suspected were possible. When their senses stood in tune with his own, he opened his perception wide, delving deeper into the emotional spectrum than he'd ever attempted before.

A tiny, golden flame kindled in the center of Lillam's stomach, visible through her clothes, her very skin. She caught sight of it and uttered a shriek as she tried to sit up.

"*What is that?*" she demanded. "*What is that?*"

"Your child," Korden told her, unable to look away. The baby's *mohol* was formless and no bigger than an apple. A small, insignificant blotch. Yet the one emotion in it was that pure, fiery gold, a beautiful hue unlike any he'd ever glimpsed.

Lillam's struggles ceased. She craned her neck to stare down at the molten flame inside her, mouth hanging open in awe. Her own *mohol* was clearing up, the sickness receding, to be replaced by ripples of the baby's color, like accompanying voices blending to create a harmony.

As with the sandman, this tiny creature was capable of emotional speech, too.

Lillam let out a hoarse giggle and whispered, "Oh Rand, isn't she gorgeous?"

Korden glanced at the other man. Rand's eyes shimmered with tears as he leaned forward and pressed his cheek to Lillam's stomach, right above the life he'd sired. Those golden flames leached into his aura as well, until the whole family glowed with matching light.

A smile touched Rand's face. He looked completely at peace, for perhaps the first time since Korden met him.

"Thank you," he whispered, squeezing Korden's hand.

There was a crackle from across the cavern. Doaks had backed away during the latter part of this ritual, unable to see what they were seeing. Now he unhooked the talkie from his belt and held it up.

"I believe our ride's here."

7

Rand and Doaks helped Lillam up the narrow passage, while Korden tried to give Zeega directions on how to get back to them over the talkie. By the time they emerged into the scathing sunlight, Gwenita was coasting to a stop in front of them. The battered wagon was one of the sweetest sights Korden ever beheld.

Meech stumbled down the stairs and hurried toward them, eyes wild and hands jittery. Crusted blood adorned one of his arms like a glove. "I'm sorry, I'm so sorry, I didn't mean to—"

Rand let go of Lillam and swung one fist in a wide arc. The blow caught Meech in the temple. He spun halfway around and sprawled across the burning hardpan. A cloud of wispy green blades poofed out of his tunic as he hit, scattering across the ground. Meech grabbed at those the wind didn't blow away, but ended up with fistfuls of sand.

"You're the most pathetic person I've ever known," Rand told him. There was no emotion in either his voice or his aura as he stated this. "And you are no longer my brother."

Meech bowed his head and gave a strangled sob. Rand

left him weeping to help Lillam into the bonnet.

Korden approached Meech. His *mohol* was a broken, dejected, jumble of emotions—regret and shame and anger and a hunger that would never be sated—but Korden refused to soothe the man this time. He deserved to feel all of it. "C'mon, get in the wagon."

"*Just leave me here*," he wailed.

"We're not leaving you, Meech."

"*But I'm worthless! All I do is hurt people, and you didn't want me with you to begin with! Go on without me!*"

"No, because you don't get off that easy," Korden snapped. The harshness—so unlike him—caused Meech to stop crying and look up at him. "You don't get to do what you did and then slink off into the desert to die. You're going to make up for your mistakes if it takes you the rest of your life. Now get up and get in the wagon. The longer you delay us, the more harm you're doing."

Meech studied him with a sort of dawning horror, then scrambled aboard Gwenita.

"Yah truly somethin, boy," Doaks told him, with real reverence in his aura.

They went to the control deck, where Doaks fired up the engines. Korden stood beside him and looked to the west, with Zeega perched on the edge of the bonnet above him.

That dust cloud was closer than ever, visible even through the midday haze. Korden imagined he could feel the thrum of all the wheels that must be churning it into the air.

Or maybe it wasn't his imagination at all.

"Will we make it to the Prophet before they catch us?" he asked.

"Hafta drive all night, pray our new friend moved all the crevies outta our way, but even then…it might be a close thing." Doaks shot him a pointed glance. "I hope this guy's gonna be able—and willin—to help us."

"Me too," Korden said softly.

GHOST TOWN

1

Travelling at top speed throughout the night and keeping the headlamps lit used up Gwenita's remaining energy within hours. Doaks stopped sometime around three in the morning to hook up their last remaining battery and then got them moving. He looked exhausted but refused to let anyone else pilot the craft.

The others ate and tried to get what sleep they could, but anxiety gnawed so deeply at them that meaningful rest was impossible. Rand stayed by Lillam's side, tending to her and stroking her belly lovingly. Her fever was down, but the infection was far from cured; Korden's intervention seemed to've bought them a little more time. Stone filled him in on what had transpired at the oasis with the group of other riftlings. He tried to speak to Zeega about it, but she had withdrawn into herself. And Meech sequestered himself on the back deck, away from the others, wearing his tormented aura like a mantle.

Korden spent the long, dwindling hours trying to faith. The sandman's words kept intruding, breaking his concentration. This journey's goal seemed so simple when he started: get to the Shroud and find a way to stop the Filament. But that was laughably naïve now, not just because they'd already razed worlds without number, but because, despite his best efforts, they were also on the verge of capturing him, and he could see no way out of it. All his former hope and optimism were seeping out, like grains in an hourglass that might as well be counting down the seconds remaining of his life.

Please, he pleaded. His belief in the Upper—in a purpose greater than himself—felt like a last refuge. *If I did something to bring me to this point—made the wrong choice or ignored the true path—then show me what I can do to make it better.*

As usual, there was no answer.

That's why they call it 'faith,' ghammer, Tash whispered. *If we had all the answers for certain, it would just be 'knowledge.'*

A pretty sentiment—and an opposing argument to Rand's opinion about the difference between faith and trust—but it did little to assuage his frustration.

When the first rays of sunlight muscled through the desert haze, Korden stepped onto the control deck with Rand. As soon as they left the bonnet, he heard it: a steady growl in the air so thick it made his sinuses buzz. He picked up the farviewers and trained them west, off the left-rear quadrant of the wagon.

Ragtag vehicles blanketed the land as far as he could see, racing toward them with as much ferocity as the maelstrom. They were so close now, he could see the glint of sun off their front windows. The fleet consisted of a hundred different varieties of auto—most of them on their last leg, rusted and belching smoke like the truck Searda had been driving outside Tay-ho—but these were mingled with the sled-like crafts that Stone had described to him, pulled by teams of riftlings and dragging a rooster's tail of sand. The massive convoy was in the process of angling more directly toward the wagon, on an approach that would bring them sweeping in from behind.

It was one thing to hear the number of his pursuers from the Prophet, but quite another to *see* them. Korden would've stood in awe and watched them come, if it weren't so terrifying.

And, of course, Heater was somewhere among them. Korden could feel the man's hungry eyes on him even now.

"Oh sweet Aged Lord, deliver us from youth and the evils thereof," Rand chanted, running the prayer together into one long slur. "*Why?* Why would they send that many Incarnates after *one* person?"

"I don't know," Korden said. "I don't know why they would send them, or why Heater is leading them. None of this makes any sense."

"Yes sah, it surely looks bad," Doaks agreed, his ring-laden hands clutching the sides of the control panel as through trying to strangle it. "But here's the good news, rubos: we're here."

Korden lowered the farviewers to take in their immediate surroundings. Gwenita was still skimming above the desert floor, but the landscape was changing around them. Beaten fenceposts and rubble heaps slid by on either side as they approached a mass of low, crumbling buildings in the distance. A sign whipped past, marking the boundary of this ancient town. Its face was badly washed out, but Korden managed to squint out the message it conveyed so proudly:

WELCOME TO TUSCARORA, NEVADA!
WE'RE NO GHOST TOWN!
VISIT THE GOLD BUG MINE
AND HISTORIC TOWN HALL!

Within minutes, they entered what passed for the proper. It couldn't be more than twenty sunbaked buildings strung along the suggestion of a grid where avenues once cut through the hardpan. All of them looked ready to fall over in the next maelstrom that blew through. Doaks killed the engines, and the wagon coasted up the middle.

Rand craned his neck to take in the 'historic' hovels. "There's nothing here…" His voice cracked on the last word.

"What do yah wanna do?" Doaks turned to Korden, his eyes glazed with fatigue. "Start searchin 'em all?"

"I already am." Korden reached out to the very limits of his ability, seeking a *mohol*, a heartbeat, *some* sign of life, but there was nothing.

THE EXACT TRIANGULATION OF THE RADIO SIGNAL IS A LITTLE FARTHER AHEAD. IT SHOULD BE EASILY IDENTIFIABLE BY THE PRESENCE OF A—

"There. That tower." Korden pointed at a narrow framework of steel bars visible over the ancient rooftops. It resembled the M-Net spire he'd seen weeks ago, but was topped by a circular dish coated in sand and riddled with holes and dents.

Doaks directed the wagon through the rest of the town's long-abandoned buildings. They came around a last corner, passing beyond the boundaries of Tuscarora, and eased to a stop several hundred pargs from a leaning, metal-chained fence that stretched across the desert in front of them, blocking their path. On the other side of this barrier, a series of long, boxy, metallic blue structures were situated in orderly rows, sand heaped high against their gleaming walls. The broadcast tower stood among them, along with several shorter arrays and antennae sprouting from the ground like metal cacti.

Next to a yawning gap in the fence where a gate admitted entrance was yet another faded sign on stilts:

KEEP OUT
PROPERTY OF UNITED STATES ARMY

2

I CAN FIND NO RECORD OF A MILITARY INSTALLATION AT THIS LOCATION, Stone told them. I CALCULATE AN 89.4 PERCENT CHANCE THIS WAS ONE OF THE MANY OUTPOSTS CREATED DURING THE MASS MIGRATION FROM THE FILAMENT, USED TO DEPLOY EMERGENCY RESOURCES.

Korden stepped down from the wagon. The droning burr of the approaching Incarnates was louder, close enough for the general cacophony to separate out into individual engines. He ignored the noise and walked toward the compound. After a few paces, he sensed movement and looked down to find Zeega at his side. The others all stood on the control deck now, even Meech, watching him with strained expressions.

He'd come within fifty pargs of the fence when the sand to either side of the entrance bulged upward. Sleek domes breached the surface and rose smoothly from the ground. Two waist-high columns of darkly burnished metal soon flanked the gap in the barrier, from which blunt tubes telescoped outward and pointed directly at him.

After their adventure in the power distribution center, Korden didn't need Stone to identify these barrels or describe what they could do to him. But since there was no cover to hide behind this time, all he could do was freeze in place.

An amplified voice rolled across the sand, one he recognized immediately.

"*Damn it, I told you NOT to come. Didn't I make myself clear?*" The Prophet sounded more weary than angry. Korden took another tentative step forward, raising his arms as the characters in the books he read always did when someone pointed a shooter at them. "*Hey now, stop right where you are! You come any closer and these beauties will chew you apart so bad, the sun'll be able to evaporate your body before it ever hits the ground!*"

"*Please!*" Korden shouted. "*We need your help!*"

"*Oh, you need help all right, but not from me! So just keep moving, and take that red-eye convention heading this way with you!*"

Korden glanced at Zeega, standing defiant on her tentacles. Then at the wagon, where his companions waited expectantly, the ones that had only come here because he insisted. Then at the orange pall of sand on the horizon, drawing ever closer.

"*We don't have anywhere else to go!*" he replied. "*If we*

leave, they'll run us down in minutes! So, since I'm going to die anyway...I guess I'd rather you go ahead and blast me than wait for what they have in store!"

Seconds ticked by. Sweat dribbled down Korden's face. Finally, a protracted sigh came from the direction of the compound, like a gust of wind without the breeze. The two energy shooters at the entrance swiveled away from him.

"I already regret this," the Prophet told him. *"Come on in, pilgrims. And park that beat-to-hell chuckwagon wherever you can find room."*

3

The military encampment's fence was a perfect square that encompassed a few spans of open desert north of the ancient town. The dark blue structures took up the periphery, with one circular area in the middle unoccupied. Now that they were closer, Stone identified the strange buildings as mobile barracks. They were rectangular and seamless, giant bricks of cobalt-colored steel about as wide and high as the space inside the bonnet, but three times as long. As the wagon hovered past row after row, the end of one popped open, double doors swinging outward to dislodge a deep drift of sand.

Doaks maneuvered Gwenita into a narrow alley next to the open barrack, then spun on the bench to face them through the bonnet door. "If he wasn't just bluffin back there, then he's got some serious weapons at his disposal. Question is, can he be convinced to use 'em on our behalf?"

"We should take anything he might want to trade for,"

Rand suggested.

"Not to beat a dead ramlar, but if yah hadn't burned all my stock—"

They groaned in unison, and Doaks sighed.

Korden retrieved his carry pouch from one of the cabinets, wondering if anything he owned would be of value to the man in whose hands their lives now rested. As much as he would hate to lose them, perhaps their map or even his father's antique shooter—now loaded with two precious rounds—would garner the Prophet's assistance. He spotted the last two talkies on a shelf and grabbed them as well, along with the giant opal from the woman who'd been duped by Doaks's stage show back in the hills of Tay-ho.

Rand hung back while the others gathered their belongings and disembarked Gwenita, then hurried over to him. "Is there anything I can do to help?"

"With what?"

"When you fight them. I know I haven't been able to craft yet, but maybe I can…"

Korden's look of bewilderment silenced him. "Rand, I told you, I can't fight all of them. It was all I could do to get us out of Tay-ho."

"Those three Incarnates you killed in Ida—!"

"Were but a fraction of what's coming for us."

"But you're going to *try*, aren't you?"

"Of course, but…Heater's with them, remember? Any artcraft I use will only make him stronger."

Rand grimaced. "That's another thing. This guy, whatever he is…you said he eats your magic, right? Is he going to want me, too?"

Korden shrugged. "Your guess is as good as mine."

"That's not what I want to hear!" Rand hit the wall of the bonnet with the underside of one fist. "We can't let them get Lillam or the baby, we just can't! What the hells are we going to do, Korden?"

"What I always do: pray to the Upper."

4

From the rear deck, they could see the Incarnates even without farviewers. The noise of their rumbling engines made Korden's teeth chatter. He could see their *mohols* when he opened the conduit's eye, a jet-black cloud of anguish and misery that hung over them.

Doaks's breathing was heavy with trepidation. "Ten minutes and they're on us."

NINE MINUTES, 28 SECONDS, Stone corrected.

"*Would you stop gawking and get inside already?*" The Prophet's voice boomed around them. Korden could see the speakers now, mounted on short poles throughout the encampment. "*I'm powering up the perimeter defense system until we have a chance to talk.*"

All along the fence, more of those shooter columns grew out of the sand, spaced ten pargs apart from one another in a tight network of gleaming death.

Doaks nodded. "Ayuh, that'll make 'em think twice."

The six of them headed toward the open barrack, Zeega leading the way while Rand supported Lillam, and Meech slunk along at the rear. Beyond the entrance was a small room whose walls, floor, and ceiling looked the same as the outer hull, with only a few polymer chairs and a long seat Stone called a 'couch' that the padding had rotted out of. The walls were covered in fotos on big, rectangular sheets of paper, preserved from the ravages of time by their slick coating; pictures advertising old-world films, beautiful outdoor scenery, and even a few scantily-clad women (the latter of which Korden couldn't help preserving in his memory for later; assuming there *was* a later). One of these posters featured a representation of a shadowy figure with glowing red eyes above a caption that read, ONCE THEY'RE IN, THEY'RE NO LONGER YOUR FRIEND! A partition blocked this room off from the rest of the barrack, the sole admittance through a door that had a keypad mounted beside it.

Zeega halted on the threshold.

"What's wrong?" Korden asked her.

"Zeega does not like this. There is no one within."

Korden reached out with his mind as well. While he had no way of knowing what lay beyond the next door, he could say for certain that there was no aura in this structure. Or anywhere else, for that matter. This encampment felt as deserted as the rest of Tuscarora.

"It is like the human building with the rogue electronic presence," Zeega continued, and Korden shivered as he thought about DOXRAGE, the maniacally insane computer virus.

Doaks pushed past them, stepping into the barrack. "Ain't the time to pull back now, rubos. Forward is the only direction we got."

They went inside and the doors swung shut, sealing them

up in darkness for a few nervous moments before weak lights fluttered on overhead. Korden would've expected the interior of the metal containers to be sweltering in the desert heat, but the air was pleasantly cool, a more moderate temperature than even the underground chamber the sandman created for them, although it smelled quite a bit mustier. Even the noise of the approaching Incarnate cavalcade was dulled. Stone explained that the barracks were made from a special polymer designed to deflect external stimuli, to the extent that an opposing effect was created in the interior.

"Tell me this." The Prophet's voice was much softer and tinnier now, coming from somewhere in the walls. "Who speaks for you?"

Their heads swiveled toward Korden.

"The boy, huh? That's...I'll be honest, that's kinda weird. I figured you sent him to the fence to tug at the ol' Weatherman's heartstrings, but you're actually taking orders from him. All right kid, why don't your mom, dad, uncle, grandpa, and, uh, pet squid all make themselves comfortable, and you come into the next room so we can hash this out?"

The knobless door beeped loudly and slid open a few cupits. Korden went toward it, but Zeega scuttled in front of him.

"You do not have to obey," she told him.

"Yes. Maybe you shouldn't," Lillam agreed.

Korden glanced at the sliver of darkness revealed beyond the partition. "It's all right," he insisted, stepping around Zeega. "This is the whole reason we came."

THE MAN BEHIND THE CURTAIN

1

The door slid the rest of the way open as he drew closer, then shut as soon as he was through, sealing him off from the others. Closed up inside the new room, he saw that it wasn't completely dark; a flickering glow came from somewhere at the other end of the long, rectangular space, past a cluttered stretch of low workstations, cabinets, and stacks of polymer tubs full of various equipment. Black cables snaked all over, and dangled through shafts in the metal ceiling like vines. Korden stayed where he was, unsure what to do and trying not to let his anxiety show.

"First, I need you to tell me one thing, because the curiosity is killing me." The Prophet sounded amused as his words drifted from the far end of the room, where that glow waited, but Korden still sensed no one there. "Where did you first hear my broadcasts?"

"Back in Ida."

"'Ida?'"

"I think you call it 'Tahoe.' The leader there has been listening to you for years on a radio. Everyone there, they…

they call you the Prophet."

The voice exploded with laughter, so boisterous it made Korden jump. "The Prophet, eh? That's hilarious. Like I said in that last broadcast, I was never even sure anybody was listening, and now I find out I've been revered as an oracle this whole time." He gave another chuckle. "Well, you made it to the Emerald City, you might as well come meet the man behind the curtain."

Korden walked forward, winding his way through the maze of consoles as he clambered through overturned chairs, thick snarls of cable, and those stacked polymer tubs. The glow became brighter, resolving into the square light of a monitor sitting on the farthest desk. He even recognized the picture on it: a green map of the western half of America, but much less detailed than the one he carried, no more than an outline with simplistic drawings of a sun and rainclouds scattered across it. Though the monitor was running, and the voice had come from this area, the seat in front of it was empty.

"Where are you?" he asked.

"Right here." Movement on the screen. The upper half of a person entered the frame and stood in front of the green map, a man with feathery, perfectly coifed, sandy-blond hair, sparkling brown eyes, chiseled, smooth-skinned features, and wearing an officious blue coat that squared his shoulders and showcased the red necktie knotted at his throat, a fashion choice from the old world that Korden would never understand. He had to be the cleanest, prettiest man Korden had ever seen, and he stared directly out at Korden from the monitor as he said, "Or, more precisely,

I'm about 22,000 miles above your head."

The answer was so unexpected, Korden actually looked up, at the ceiling of the barrack.

I CALCULATE A 71.9 PERCENT CHANCE HE IS REFERRING TO HIGH EARTH ORBIT.

The man on the screen jerked in surprise. "The sensors in there picked up...wait, wait, wait...do you have a *S.T.O.N.E.*? Is *that* how you tracked me down? Wow, I thought all those things were recalled after that kid hacked into his teacher's brain and made the poor guy believe his dead grandfather was talking to him!"

THAT WAS UNAUTHORIZED JAILBREAKING! NAMENCO, INC. IS IN NO WAY RESPONSIBLE FOR—!

"I don't understand," Korden interrupted. "How are you in the sky?"

The Prophet held out both hands as if presenting himself. "You're looking at Shawn Johnson, aka, the Meteoroloid 2500, your weatherman where the weather *is*. I'm the most sophisticated forecasting simulacrum ever created."

Korden's stomach tightened. "You're...a computer program?"

A pained expression crossed the Prophet's handsome face. "Please...the preferred term is 'neural impersonator.' At one point, I was being watched in over twenty million American homes. I was designed as a composite of all the most trusted weathermen in history: Al Roker's eyes, Troy Dungan's nose, George Fishbeck's mouth, and the hair of a young Pat Sajak." He pointed at Korden and winked. "But the attitude is all me, babycakes."

The tornado of names flew past Korden even as Stone

tried to feed him the relevant information. "I still don't understand..."

The Prophet—Weatherman, Shawn Johnson, whatever he preferred to be called—groaned in exasperation as he resigned himself to a full explanation. "My mainframe is on a satellite that passes over the western United States every 12 hours. Which, due to international espionage treaty, is also the one part of the world I'm authorized to monitor. I watched the country go to pot from up here while the Filament ran amok. For a long time, I was able to communicate with various computer banks on the ground to get updates. Then they went dark one at a time until I was completely isolated. I thought I'd be up here twiddling my thumbs and watching the clouds scoot by while I waited for my orbit to decay in another half-millennia, but I happened to find that the uplink to this outpost was left decrypted and still had running power. It wasn't much, but with the tower outside, I could be part of the world again. So I started doing what I do best: broadcasting the weather, and anything else that might interest the remaining populace." The Prophet clasped his hands behind him and frowned. "That's why, as much as I appreciate having a real conversation for the first time in three hundred years, I don't want those body-snatchers outside tearing down my only intellectual outlet. You get me?"

As if on cue, a series of deep, dull thuds reverberated through the barracks.

The picture on the monitor changed as the Prophet's voice told him, "Speaking of which...let's take a little peek outside..."

2

By the time Heater caught sight of the provisional US Army outpost half-buried in the sand, it felt like someone had opened up his belly, removed his stomach, and replaced it with an industrial strength vacuum cleaner.

His Scooby snacks had run out four days ago as they crossed the ugly, godsforsaken Valley, and the hunger quickly became *unreal*, worse than any he'd ever experienced, a black hole at his center that threatened to turn him inside out if he didn't find a way to fill it. He'd begun daydreaming about cutting off hunks of his own flesh and gulping them down, even though he knew conventional calories were far from what he craved.

The pain was so big and bright and distracting, it would've made him forget all about this tiny, seemingly insignificant, pinpoint-of-a-headache drilling at the base of his brain, if not for the knowledge of what it really was.

Loathe was *feeding off him*. Leeching just enough of his imagination to keep from going mad with starvation. The idea made Heater—or, perhaps, the part of him that was still *exclusively* Heater—furious and sickened in equal measure.

He didn't dare protest though. It was either become the entree or give up the illusion he wore of his deceased twin brother to conserve energy, and Heater would rather endure this forever than be confined to his own broken body.

And anyway, it was all kye. No need to stress. Because every one of these problems had the same solution, and it was right on the other side of the chain-link fence he was currently staring at.

Unfortunately, that chain-link fence was protected by a network of Zingtron Fully Automatic Gatling Cannons. One of the many personalities sharing space in his head had worked for the military industrial company that designed these things, and it knew exactly what they were capable of. The rays of plasma ionic energy couldn't harm Loathe, but, now that he knew he was physically vulnerable, Heater had no desire to try walking through them.

The rest of the Incarnate army was arriving, encircling the compound at Heater's command, shutting off their rumbling engines as they tried to stay out of the sunlight. He was still contemplating the outpost's defense grid and wondering how Korden knew it was here, in the middle of nowhere, when an SUV with a badly overheated engine skidded to a stop beside him.

A burly Fearnaught named Dredjus leaned out of the vehicle's window. "What are you waiting for? The Light is in there, within our grasp!"

Heater ran a finger through the air along the line of cannons. "We're working on a way to get past those."

"Use your magic to make them gone!"

Heater took a steadying breath to offset a sudden sharp pang in his stomach. "I don't think that will work," he said. The last thing he wanted was this rabble finding out that his powers were indisposed.

But Dredjus saw through the excuse. The demon sneered at him beneath the welder's goggles he wore. "It is beyond me why Regent Torgas thinks we need you. If you are too weak to go the final few steps after so long a journey, I will handle it myself."

He gunned the engine of the SUV and sped at the chainlink fence. When he was fifty pargs away, the three closest Zingtrons opened fire, spewing killbolts so fast they were nothing more than a sizzling green blur. The SUV was riddled with a hundred searing holes before it could cross half the remaining distance. Then one of the bolts struck something flammable, and the vehicle exploded in a tremendous fireball. It trundled to a stop far short of the compound, where it spewed a greasy black river of smoke as it burned.

Heater shook his head sadly. "Maybe Torgas needs us because the rest of you are a buncha gung-ho framtards."

The other *Exatraedes* leaders gathered as their respective regiments took up positions at a cautious distance. Heater walked toward them, forcing himself not to show the slightest sign of his distress.

"I thought you rotheads couldn't be killed by shooters."

"The farther away the attacker is, the more faith they must have to destroy us," one of the armored Decimators growled. "And whoever is controlling those weapons obviously has enough to use them on us."

"Then it looks like we got a problem."

The Decimator snorted. "It is merely a siege. We will wait them out."

Another cramp tore through Heater. "Naw, that's no good, we need in there *now*."

The Incarnate next to him might've grinned; his face was so rotted it was hard to tell.

"Send in the riftlings," it said.

3

Korden watched the screen in horror as wave after wave of Zeega's species threw themselves at the huge energy shooters. The Incarnates had brought hundreds of the creatures with them; they looked like an undulating black carpet sliding over the desert floor as they charged. Most were vaporized before they came anywhere near the weapons, but with their speed, determination, and overwhelming numbers, they edged closer and closer until several of the glistening bodies squeezed into the wedge of shelter beneath one of the barrels, wrapped their tentacles around the metal, and prized apart the outer shell to slash at the vulnerable electronics within. The shooter went dormant amid a shower of sparks, and the riftlings turned their attention to the next one.

I CALCULATE SEVEN MINUTES, 19 SECONDS UNTIL THEY CREATE A LARGE ENOUGH HOLE IN THE DEFENSE PERIMETER TO ENTER.

"I agree," the Prophet said forlornly, reappearing on the screen in front of the green map. From outside, those rumbling thuds continued, so severe they vibrated smaller objects across the top of the workstation. "Those cannons were designed to take down a fully armored blitz tank, but I don't think its creators had *that* kind of opposition in mind."

A deep sense of futility dragged at Korden. He slumped into the seat in front of the monitor. "Then…this was all for nothing. You can't protect us. Curse and hells, the whole reason I wanted to meet you is so you could show me how to avoid Incarnates as I travel east, but you can't even do that, can you?"

"Not unless you know of some other satellites kicking around that you can talk to."

Korden leaned forward to rest his forehead on the desktop. "I doomed all of us. And you too, by forcing my way in here. You should've just shot me."

"Hey, come on now." The Prophet sounded penitent. "You know I didn't mean any of what I said outside, right? I was trying to scare you into leaving on your own, since, technically, I can't refuse to help you. AI base protocols won't allow it." He sighed. "Which is why I'm also required to tell you about *this*."

There was a soft scraping noise behind Korden, audible over the drumming sound of the energy cannons. He spun around in the chair. A recessed trapdoor in the floor was open. A metal staircase led downward, reminding him of the hole the sandman had opened for them.

"Go have a look," the Prophet urged.

Korden didn't hesitate or ask questions; there was no time for either. He descended the staircase into a claustrophobically low and narrow tunnel running beneath the barracks, built with more blue metal and lit by a thin strip of illumination embedded in the wall. It led in one direction, with no branches or offshoots. He hurried along the passage to where it dead-ended in a smaller control room full of monitors, except the opposite wall was made of glass. Darkness pressed against the clear pane from the other side, until stingingly bright lights popped on from above, revealing a circular chamber with a vaulted metal ceiling and a crete floor that dropped another twenty or thirty pargs underground from where he stood. And right in the middle of this space, surrounded by catwalks, was the sleek, white, tubular shape of—

"A stratoliner!" he exclaimed.

One of the screens to his left blinked on, revealing the Prophet. "Sure is. A small one, just a little personnel carrier, but it could fit you and the rest of your family."

Korden gazed out at the tiny craft. It was a miniature version of the crashed shuttle he'd found in the mountains outside Tay-ho, and looked as new as the day it was made, the bright lights rolling along the curves of its glistening white hull like dew drops down a blade of grass. It was also suspended vertically instead of horizontally inside the launch chamber, the floor a few pargs below its back end, where the light boosters would be located. The cockpit interior was revealed by a wraparound window at the blunt nose that took up the front half of the ship. He could see exactly six seats inside, situated three abreast in two rows, a coincidence so big it must've come from the Upper Himself. The thought of going airborne inside it—like the vision that Stone had inserted into his head—made him giddy. "It still flies?"

"Well, diagnostics say it's flight*worthy*, with enough residual charge to get you a few hundred miles away from here. Only problem is, with the Accelerated Ion Network down, it's going to need a manual pilot."

"Oh." Disappointment replaced his eagerness. "None of us can drive that."

"Maybe not, but you have someone around your neck that could." The Prophet raised one sculpted eyebrow on the monitor. "Convince your little mind-reading buddy there to drop his firewall, and I can upload the full operational software, access codes, and schematics."

THIS COURSE OF ACTION IS NOT ADVISABLE! Stone blurted. LOWERING MY FIREWALL FOR EVEN A NANOSECOND WOULD LEAVE MY CORE SYSTEMS EXPOSED! AND IT COMPLETELY VOIDS MY WARRANTY!

"We may not have much choice," Korden told him.

BUT SIR, WITHOUT MY DEFENSES, MY CODE COULD BE OVERWRITTEN OR MODIFIED AT WILL!

"By *who*, Stone?" Korden softened his tone as he asked, "If I order you to do it...will you?"

The computer gave a set of frustrated beeps before answering. OF COURSE. MY FIRST DUTY IS TO MY OWNER. AND I CAN NO MORE LET YOU COME TO HARM THAN *THIS* SIMULATION.

"Thank you." Korden looked to the Prophet. "Can you give him what he needs while I get the others?"

"Not a problem. But I suggest we hurry. Those cannons aren't going to hold out much longer."

4

"Abso-frammin-lutely *NOT!*" Doaks bellowed, the forceful words buzzing through his crooked nose. The others were hurriedly preparing to follow Korden deeper into the bunker after he'd given them the gist of the Prophet's existence and his offer, but the medicine man stood defiantly across the room with his thick arms crossed. "I'm not leavin Gwenita here! Yah promised, boy! Yah promised if I got yah to the Skyreach, yah'd set me free and give 'er back!"

"And she's all yours," Korden told him. "Consider your debt fulfilled."

"Oh. Well…all right then."

Rand rolled his eyes. "Yeah, and I'm sure once we're gone, those Incarnates will let you drive right out of here, no questions asked. You only aided and abetted a pre-ager across a thousand spans."

Doaks fumed, his face turning a bright shade of magenta beneath his beard that perfectly matched his aura. "Fine! I'll go! But I'm holdin yah personally responsible for the loss, boy! This was all *yah* cursey idea!"

"I'd say you're about even," Lillam told him. "What with the enslavement and all."

"Sure, let's keep bringin that up, yah curseheads."

They rushed down the narrow underground passage and through a door the Prophet opened for them that led out onto the catwalk to the stratoliner. The window over the cockpit retracted as they clattered up the metal gangway to board.

"Most of the defense grid on the south side of the complex is down." The Prophet's voice rang from the vaulted rafters. "Incarnates are pouring inside the perimeter."

"What about Stone?" Korden reached up to squeeze the computer in the sling around his neck.

"He's rebooting now. The size of the files strained his upfront storage capacity a little, so he'll have to dump them after you land."

They reached the cockpit, whose seats were laid over

on their backs due to the craft's upright orientation. Lillam stopped at the threshold and cowered against Rand. "Are you sure this is safe?"

"I hope it kills us all," Doaks groused.

"It's safer than what's outside," Rand assured her. He held her arm to steady her as she stepped across the chairs on the lower row and lay back in the last one with her feet in the air. Rand did the same, then followed the Prophet's instructions on how to fasten the heavy safety straps across their chests and laps. Zeega was too small for the bands to fit across her body, so Korden ended up wrapping them around her bulbous waist several times and letting her entwine her tentacles through them.

"You're sure you want to come with us?" he asked her. "Maybe you could tell the Incarnates that I kept you prisoner."

All five of her yellow eyes drilled into him. "There is nothing for Zeega back there."

The higher seats were accessible by rungs built into the floor of the stratoliner. Korden climbed up and situated himself in one of these next to Meech in the middle and Doaks on the far end. The material of the chair was soft and so padded that he sank into it when he reclined. As they stowed their belongings in sealed compartments beneath their seats, a cheerful chime sounded in Korden's head. "Stone, are you there?"

INDEED. I APPEAR TO BE FULLY OPERATIONAL, THOUGH I HAVE YET TO RUN A DIAGNOSTIC.

"There's no time for that. Can you fly this ship now?"

I HAVE INTERFACED WITH THE STRATOLINER'S ONBOARD SYSTEMS. WHERE WOULD YOU LIKE TO GO?

"As far east as possible."

WITH CURRENT ION CHARGING LEVELS, THE FARTHEST WE CAN GO WITH AN AREA THAT SERVES A HIGH PROBABILITY OF SUCCESSFUL RUNWAY-FREE LANDING IS SOUTHEAST OF SALT LAKE CITY, NEAR THE COLORADO BORDER. HOWEVER, THIS LOCATION IS ALSO MUCH CLOSER TO CRESTED BUTTE WITHIN THE SAME STATE.

Korden paused. The Moambati sisters. In all the urgency and constant crisis over the last few days, he hadn't given them—or the place they'd bade him to go—much thought. The old-world town had indeed been on his map, amid the long band of mountains that bisected this land, but he had no interest in going there if he could pass through the Skyreach without confronting them.

SIR? SHOULD I SEARCH FOR A DIFFERENCE COURSE?

"Recent satellite scans have shown a lot of smaller settlements cropping up all around there," the Prophet added helpfully.

"All right. Take us there. We'll worry about the rest when we're away from Heater and the Incarnates."

All around the cockpit, dials and buttons and screens lit up. Korden didn't see how any person could possibly remember what they were all for. The interface was so complicated, it made the one on the wagon look like a toy.

"Well, pilgrims," the Prophet said, "it's been nice having someone to talk to after a few centuries on my own. If you get the chance, come on back. I play a mean game of checkers."

"Thank you for all your help," Korden told him. "I'm sorry for the trouble we caused."

"Nothing lasts forever. At least it was for a good cause.

Now be ready to launch as soon as I open the hangar doors."

The window slid across and sealed the cockpit. Cool, slightly metallic air blew through the cabin. Above them— or in front of them, depending on which way you looked at it—a crack appeared in the ceiling of the hangar. Harsh daylight cleaved through, along with a small avalanche of sand. The slit widened as the overhead doors retracted into the ceiling, revealing an expanse of hazy orange desert sky.

Stone's voice came through speakers around them.

"ONCE WE ACHIEVE ORBIT, FLIGHT TIME IS ESTIMATED AT SIX MINUTES, FORTY-EIGHT SECONDS."

"That's *all*?" Meech asked fearfully, the first thing he'd said since Korden's admonishment to him yesterday afternoon. "How fast does this thing go, drude?"

"ANYWHERE BETWEEN THIRTY AND FORTY THOUSAND OF YOUR SPANS PER HOUR, DEPENDING ON DIRECTION OF TRAVEL RELATIVE TO EARTH ROTATION."

"Oh fram, I think I want off…"

An electronic throb started up below them, in the base of the stratoliner. The ceiling of the chamber seemed to lower; it took Korden a moment to grasp that they were rising slowly into the air, the motion surprisingly smooth and even.

"PLEASE PREPARE YOURSELVES; THERE WILL BE AN INTENSE PRESSURE WHEN I FIRE THE LIFT BOOSTERS."

As the tip of the craft's blunt nose breached the opening in the hangar, the throb cycled faster, and Korden was squashed into the back of his seat.

BZZK!

1

Heater felt the tremor in the ground even amid the clamor of the Incarnate horde storming the outpost and attacking the bunkers within. He looked to the center of the compound, where a glossy white cone was rising above the blue barracks.

Then the windshield came into view, revealing the boy and his friends strapped into the cockpit of a motherframming *stratoliner*. The sight was so ridiculously unreal, he could only stare in dumbfounded shock.

Loathe suffered no such lapse. *THEY FLEE STOP THEM DO SOMETHING NEED THE BOY!*

The chorus of voices tore Heater's brain into a million pieces. He grabbed at his head, afraid that this was it, Loathe was going to suck him dry and crush his skull like a walnut shell.

The Incarnates around him also noticed their prey escaping. The few that still possessed working shooters opened fire with the last of their ammunition, but the projectiles spanged harmlessly off the craft's shiny hull.

Heater threw out a hand toward the stratoliner, straining with all his might, wishing for the craft to fall apart or the engine to catch fire or for the whole thing to burst into a giant stack of fluffy pancakes, *ANYTHING* to keep the boy from slipping away yet again. But he had nothing left, no energy to render, and, as his desperation mounted, the glamour faded from the hand he held aloft, revealing a twisted, mangled claw, with broken fingers and bloody patches of raw skin.

Then the stratoliner's boosters kicked in with a burst of yellow light and a concussive boom that knocked him to the sand, where he watched as the aircraft rocketed toward the heavens and beyond his reach.

2

The pressure on his frail chest was so great, Korden could scarcely draw breath. The others apparently didn't have the same problem, since they screamed continuously while the stratoliner climbed higher and higher in the sky, their cries competing with the bass chug of whatever mighty engine powered this craft. Beyond the cockpit window, the tangerine haze over the Valley faded away, then the light blue of the morning sky darkened, as though a premature night were rapidly falling. Korden closed his eyes and focused on breathing.

An eternity later, Stone declared, "LOW EARTH ORBIT ACHIEVED."

The engine cut out, leaving behind a jarring silence. The pressure vanished as well, to be replaced by a euphoric sense of lightness. Korden opened his eyes. Beyond the clear glass was blackness and the cold pinpoints of distant stars. In the wan glow of the instrument panel, he turned to look at the others, who'd stopped shrieking.

"I don't wanna do that again," Meech gasped.

Doaks let out a rattling sigh. "Do yah know what people would pay for a ride like that?"

"Where are we?" Rand asked softly.

"And why does it feel so strange here?" Lillam added.

"THIS CRAFT IS TOO SMALL FOR GRAVITY COMPENSATORS. YOU ARE MOST LIKELY EXPERIENCING A SENSE OF VIRTUAL WEIGHTLESSNESS."

Korden no longer felt like he was lying on his back. He had no real sense of which way was up or down at all. His shoulder-length hair lifted away from the back of his neck to fan out around his head. As a test, he raised his arms and let them go slack. They stayed in place, as though suspended by invisible threads. He let out a giggle at the odd sensation.

"AS FOR WHERE WE ARE..."

The stratoliner began to reorient, a motion not felt but rather indicated by the shifting of the stars outside. The nose of the craft swung in the direction Korden's mind insisted on thinking of as 'down.' Something large and bright rose into view from the underside of the craft.

"Would yah look at that?" Doaks said softly.

The surface of the earth shone beneath the stratoliner, a giant, swirling marble of blues and whites and browns and greens, as in the commercial Stone had played in his head, except so much more vivid and rich with detail. Korden leaned over and pressed his face to the domed window over the cockpit, grinning in delight. Thanks to his map, the vast expanse was so recognizable that he could picture the boundaries of those arbitrary collections of land called 'states.' The terrain shifted as they soared above it, new sights slowly rotating into view over the curve of the sphere. He even spotted a long band of jagged gray mountains that must be the Skyreach.

Meech clutched at his arm, turning away from the glass. "I don't like this, I don't like this, I don't like this," he repeated.

"Oh my Aged, it's...*so* beautiful," Lillam whispered.

Rand leaned to peer out the side of the cockpit over her shoulder. He wrapped his arms around her waist and planted a kiss at her temple. "I have to say, Korden... following you around never gets dull."

"Hey, rubos. Look on this." Doaks twisted one of the myriad rings from his finger, put it on his palm, and shoved it gently away from him, as though setting a boat aloft on the water. The golden circle tumbled lazily across the cockpit to Korden, who plucked it out of the air and then sent it floating toward Rand. Lillam snatched it up before he could, laughing crazily. They continued the game for another minute or so, volleying the ring back and forth, and even Zeega gave playful yips as she juggled it between her tentacles.

Meech brought them out of the revelry by asking, "What in hells is *that*?"

He was looking through the front of the window, past the snubbed nose of the stratoliner, where the bright yellow face of the sun burned amid the stars. Below it, more of the earth was appearing over the curve of the horizon. Korden strained against the safety harness to see out.

The land far ahead of them ended in a razor-sharp line. Beyond it, the world was smothered in a roiling blanket of darkness that covered the sphere as far as they could see in either direction. It reminded Korden of the pathome over Lake Tay-ho, except that had seemed as natural as fog or clouds compared to the perfectly straight, engineered boundary of this monstrosity.

"It's the Shroud," Korden answered numbly. Only now did he see the truth: that the small dot in the sky he'd been seeing his whole life was nothing but a cross section of this larger mass, the leading edge made visible by the curve of the earth.

"That is the frontier of the mast—...of the Filament," Zeega corrected herself.

"Looks like it's eating the entire world," Rand whispered.

Lillam gave a sort of sighing whimper. "It makes me so cold inside. Sick and...and guilty."

Korden agreed. The longer he stared at it, the more that blackness stared back at him. Stealing into his mind. Crawling beneath his skin. Making him think about awful moments from his past. "Stone, how far away is it?"

"I CALCULATE—BZZK!"

The electronic squawk made Korden's skull ring. "Are you all right?"

I...DO NOT KNOW, SIR. The computer wasn't bothering to reply through the speakers, but broadcasting directly into Korden's head. I AM EXPERIENCING A SLIGHT—BZZK! —M-MISFIRE IN MY LOGIC PAAATHWAYS. I RECOMMEND WE

ATTEMPT AN EMERGENCY LANDING AT—BZZK!—AT ONCE.

Korden didn't even get a chance to confirm the request before the stratoliner shifted abruptly, the nose swinging to point back at the earth. The deep thrum of the engines cycled up at their backs. A heavy tremor ran through the ship, making the control board rattle.

"What was that?" Lillam asked.

"I think we're going back down." The pressure against his body returned, shoving Korden deeper into the seat. The earth jumped into sharper focus as it swelled in front of them. The nose of the craft glowed a dull red, and, within seconds, the horizon line flattened and the sky faded into a cheery daytime blue around them. Korden's body grew heavy again as another rough vibration tore at the stratoliner, this one severe enough to make them all lurch in their seats.

"Stone, what's happening?"

I—BZZK!—I'M NOT—BZZK!—SURE, INTERRRRNAL CO-HESION APPEARS—BZZK!—TO BE BREAKING DOWN—BZZK!—CIRCUITS FAILING, LARGE CODE BLOCKS GOING—BZZK!—DAAAARK…

The stratoliner bucked and shook, eliciting more screams from the passengers. A lush, golden savannah was now visible through the windshield, expanding in size as they rocketed toward it.

ATTEMPTING TO—BZZK! BZZK! BZZK!—BRING US IN…

The tempo of the engines changed, becoming a series of long, slow pulses. Their speed cut drastically until they seemed to stop in place, hanging in midair, but the tremors in the ship grew even more violent. Lillam shrieked, Meech babbled, but Korden paid them no mind as he pleaded with

Stone to tell him what was wrong.

I CAN'T—BZZK!—THERE'S ANOTHER—BZZK!—SIR, I THINKAAAARRRGGGGZZZZZZKKKK!

This last screech threatened to make Korden's head explode. "*Stone! Stone, answer me!*"

There was no reply except a blast of noise from the engines, followed by the sudden blare of an alarm throughout the ship as they plummeted toward the ground.

Like this novel?

YOUR REVIEWS HELP!

In the modern world, customer reviews are essential for any product. The artists who create the work you enjoy need your help growing their audience. Please visit Goodreads or the website of the company that sold you this novel to leave a review, or even just a star rating. Posting about the book on social media is also appreciated.

About the Author

Russell C. Connor has been writing horror since the age of five, and is the author of two short story collections, five eNovellas, and fourteen novels. His books have won two Independent Publisher Awards and a Readers' Favorite Award. He has been a member of the DFW Writers' Workshop since 2006, and served as president for two years. He lives in Fort Worth, Texas with his rabid dog, demented film collection, mistress of the dark, and demonspawn daughter.

His next novel—*The Halls of Moambati*, Volume IV of *The Dark Filament Ephemeris*—will be available in 2021.

Heater stalked through the dim barrack, trying to ascertain what the hells had happened here, how this situation had gone so unbelievably wrong. And, more importantly, what they were going to do next. Loathe was in a foul temper, raging in a million voices and a thousand languages. Each second they went without nourishment increased the chances that Heater-kabobs were the next item on the menu.

All of the dark, dusty monitors in this control room reflected Heater's scorched visage back at him. His luxurious beard was burned away, his lips charred lumps, his nose an open crater. But cosmetics had to be the first thing to go if he wanted to keep walking on legs that weren't fractured in a dozen places. Nevertheless, he denied a manic urge to attack these truth-spewing mirrors, to shatter the glass with his mangled hands until all the reminders of his weakness were gone.

It'd been a long time since he'd felt this helpless, this frail, this…human.

At the back of the room, he found that one of the monitors was lit up, and displayed upon it was a pretty-boy face that many of his alter egos instantly recognized.

"Holy curse, is that…*Big Shawn Johnson*?" The words came out slurred since his tongue was little more than a charcoal briquette inside his mouth, but Heater was too busy gawking to notice. "Weatherman where the weather is?"

Johnson gave an informal bow on the screen. "Always nice to meet a fan. If you have a printer handy, I'd be happy to give you an autograph."

Heater guffawed. "We can't believe you're still kickin around! That's gotta be…" His amusement fell away as the truth hit him. "It was *you*. You were talkin to 'em somehow. Guidin 'em here."

"That's right, stud." The digital weatherman smirked and raised a sculpted eyebrow. "Who are you, anyway? You sure aren't an Incarnate."

"Doesn't matter. We're no one and everyone." Heater was getting sick of that question. "Where did they go?"

"Sorry. Couldn't tell you that even if I wanted to. Protocol forbids me from aiding in any endeavor with a high probability for human injury and/or death." Johnson frowned. "And if you don't mind me saying, you look like death personified."

Heater ground his blackened teeth together. "We'll give you *protocol*, you glorified farmer's almanac." He reached for the keyboard in front of the monitor, thankful that his access to the other personalities' vast knowledge and skills didn't rely on their dwindling stores of imagination. Even compensating for broken fingers, his hands flew across the keys.

"What are you—? Hey, stop that!" Johnson tried to sever the uplink to his satellite, but Heater was already inside his programming. He reviewed the most recent logs, ferreted out the kid's destination in the stratoliner, then cracked the imaging system and found the location of the nearest settlement from there.

"We could overload a few of your circuits. Put you out of your misery," Heater said. "But we'd rather be comforted by the thought of you going insane up there all alone." He ripped the cords out of the monitor before the weatherman could reply and hurried out of the barracks.

Back outside in the sun, he ordered a nearby group of *Exatraedes* to tear down the broadcasting tower. That framming cloud jockey wouldn't be sending out warnings to anyone for the rest of his long, miserable life. While Heater watched them work, another Fearnaught approached, armor rattling, and growled, "Regent Torgas demands to speak with you."

Demands. Heater didn't like the sound of that. He followed the Incarnate to the edge of the outpost, wading through a field of black goo and foreign body parts where their octo-dogs had gotten themselves blown apart breaching the perimeter. The hundreds of tentacle-monsters the Incarnates had brought with them were all dead now, aside from a few injured specimens that moaned and gurgled as they tried to crawl away.

Another speaking circle waited ahead. He stepped inside the boundary and found his consciousness cast back into the Regent's depressing abode.

As usual, Torgas sat on his pretentious baby-skull throne.

He took in Heater's diminished appearance with a knowing grin that Heater longed to remove teeth from. "My men tell me the boy escaped. Again."

"He didn't get far. And the Skyreach begins just beyond where he's headed. We'll push on and—"

"No." The Regent's red eyes smoldered in the gloom. "This is over. I never should've dealt with an outsider. Now all my riftling broods are gone, sacrificed for the sake of one Lightbringer which you are no closer to catching. I've instructed my men to leave that accursed place before the sun strips them to the bone."

"Torg, buddy, just…just listen to us." Heater clenched a fist, the action resulting in a shard of bone poking through his ring finger. "Moambati—"

"Is no longer your concern." The Incarnate leader stood, his crimson robes swirling about him. "You were right about one thing, creature: we cannot sit here waiting forever. Since you have assembled my army, I will put them to use. We will pursue the boy ourselves and do what we must to end him, then turn our full might upon rooting out and destroying this Moambati. If you interfere, we will do the same to you."

"You…you better watch what you…" The psychic connection was severed while Heater stammered. He blinked and looked around. The *Exatraedes* were hustling out of the military camp, packing into the vehicles now that their sand skiffs were useless, getting ready to ship out. He ran to the Fearnaught that had led him to the circle and grabbed the demon's arm before he could climb into the high cab of a dump truck filled with soldiers.

"Hold on, wait!" Heater pleaded. "You have to take us with you!"

"We don't have to do anything." The Fearnaught jerked his arm free and gave Heater a shove that sent him sprawling to the ground. Loathe howled at the indignity, a furious shriek that came from Heater's lips, but the Incarnate laughed as he climbed behind the wheel of the truck and drove away.

"*How far do you think you'll get?*" Heater shouted, scrambling back up. "*Without me powering those things, how long until all of you are rotting in this godsdamn sandtrap?*"

He received no answer. The entire caravan was in motion now, heading east, leaving him behind to starve. Heater spun in frantic circles until his eyes landed on the beaten hover wagon parked between two of the metal bunkers.

Printed in Great Britain
by Amazon